MAN FROM PINE RIDGE

MAN FROM PINE RIDGE

by

J. P. O'Donnell

Dales Large Print Books
Long Preston, North Yorkshire,
BD23 4ND, England.

British Library Cataloguing in Publication Data.

O'Donnell, J. P.
    Man from Pine Ridge.

    A catalogue record of this book is
    available from the British Library

    ISBN   978-1-84262-510-1 pbk

First published in Great Britain in 2006 by Robert Hale Ltd.

Cover illustration © Gordon Crabb by arrangement with
Alison Eldred

Published in Large Print 2007 by arrangement with
Robert Hale Limited

Dales Large Print is an imprint of Library Magna Books Ltd.

Printed and bound in Great Britain by
T.J. (International) Ltd., Cornwall, PL28 8RW

1

The tall, dark lawman gripped the worn hitching-post and finished tying up his black stallion, when a loud shout broke the stillness of the hot afternoon.

'Sheriff Roberts! Sheriff Roberts!' rang out down the street. Rush Roberts's head snapped in the direction of the voice. He ran his hand through his thick, black hair and watched old man Nelson scuttle down the sidewalk.

'Ole Svenson sent me to get you!' Nelson explained breathlessly as he drew abreast the lawman. 'You better get over to the blacksmith shop quick.' Nelson bent over to catch his breath and added: 'White Elk's going to kill Frank Gerard.'

Roberts's brown eyes flashed in the afternoon sunlight. He jumped onto the wide wooden sidewalk and ran down the street towards Svenson's blacksmith shop. He unsnapped the rawhide tie around the trigger of his Colt .45 as he dodged two women on their way into Jay's emporium. His long,

7

muscular legs worked in smooth rhythm.

Rush Roberts realized that White Elk would be a handful. He had had confrontations with the big Indian before and knew White Elk was as short-tempered as a cornered wolverine. Everyone in town knew White Elk and avoided the big Indian as much as possible, but Frank Gerard was always looking for a fight.

Rush wondered what had happened this time. Gerard had probably opened his big mouth and said something that didn't set well with White Elk. That wasn't very smart. Everyone in town knew White Elk could bend iron bars with his bare hands. Roberts hoped he'd get there in time.

The lawman rounded the last corner and spotted a group of cowboys huddled in front of Svenson's blacksmith shop. Nothing moved except three saddle-ponies tied up in front, their tails slapping flies.

Inside Svenson's, standing twenty feet apart, two grim-faced men faced each other. One of them, scraggly bearded Frank Gerard, leveled his pistol at the other man. White Elk, a long piece of pig-iron held tightly in his hands, stood up against one of Svenson's anvils. His eyes shone with a fierce animal-like look.

Roberts yanked out his Colt .45, thumbed the trigger back and halted ten steps from Gerard's side.

'Drop the gun, Frank,' he growled. Gerard stood still, his cold blue eyes fixed on White Elk's midsection.

Gerard snapped at the sheriff:

'I ain't doing no such thing until I teach this Injun a lesson.'

'Sheriff, he's just mad because I said howdy to his girl,' White Elk snapped. 'I'm a man same as him and can say what I want. I was just trying to be sociable. Besides, I haven't had a drink all morning.'

Rush Roberts took a long breath.

'Frank, drop the gun,' he repeated, his voice firm and controlled.

'It's just like you to stick up for your dirty Injun friends,' Gerard snorted. 'You ain't got the guts to kill me, lawman.'

'You pull that trigger and I'll put a slug in the back of your head. It might make things a little messy in here, but that's OK with me.'

'His kind shouldn't be talking to any white woman.'

'You don't want to make a problem about her do you, Frank? What's the real problem?'

9

'OK, I'll tell you what's eating me,' Gerard snapped. 'You're right, maybe he didn't mean anything by saying hello to that woman, but there's something else. We've been losing a lot of cattle the last two months, as many as ten at a time, and I think it's his kind doing the thieving.'

'You're a liar,' White Elk yelled.

Gerard continued: 'I'm a liar? If I'm lying, then how come we found Sioux arrows sticking out of our steers on White Clay Creek? I figured you killed the ones that couldn't travel fast.'

Roberts kept his pistol pointed at Gerard's temple.

'What about it, White Elk? Any truth to what he says?'

'You aren't going to believe him are you, Roberts? He's just a stinking Injun. Wait a minute, now I understand. I almost forgot you're an Injun too,' Gerard snarled.

Roberts's eyes flashed and his jaw clenched, making his high cheekbones even more pronounced. He was Pawnee and proud of it.

'You're pushing it, Frank,' he said. 'Tell me your side, White Elk.'

'Sure we've been on the Big A before, seeing we don't have a choice. It's the only way we can get to the reservation. I'll admit to that, but we never took any beef. I've seen bones along the creek, but I figured they were coyote kills. Someone might be stealing cattle, but it isn't me.'

'I don't care what he says,' shouted Gerard. 'Mr Appleton pays me to protect his property and I say it's his bunch rustling and butchering our cattle.' Gerard glared at White Elk.

'I figure you're going to stick up for your own kind and not arrest him,' he continued. 'Let him come at me with that pig-iron and we'll see what happens.'

'Frank,' shouted Roberts, 'If you pull that trigger, I'll kill you.'

Gerard's fury blinded him to the sheriff's threat. Without warning, he snapped off a shot at White Elk, but missed. Almost immediately Roberts's Colt roared, and the heavy slug crashed through Gerard's head, sending him crashing against a wooden support post holding up the building. He was dead before he hit the ground.

Roberts walked over to the crumpled man. A pool of blood spread out from under the dead foreman's head. The Pawnee's face was tight.

'Right through the head, Sheriff,' ventured

one of the cowboys. 'That's mighty fine shooting.'

Roberts stared at the corpse.

'You didn't have any choice,' spoke up old man Harper, 'He would have killed you sure as I'm standing here.'

Robert's eyes scanned the faces of the cowboys.

'Take him over to the Clays' funeral parlor and clean up this mess,' he said. 'Make sure you tell Clay to keep him until he hears from me or Appleton.'

'You bet, Sheriff.'

The cowboys dragged Gerard's lifeless body from the building and took him over to the funeral parlor. In the meantime Svenson took a shovel and spread some charcoal ashes from the fire-pit on the ground where Frank had fallen, his head split open like a ripe melon.

Roberts turned to White Elk. 'You better head for home. It's all over.'

'I never much cared for you Roberts, you being a lawman and all. We're having a hard time on the reservation. I figured you didn't much care about your own kind, Pawnee or Sioux. Maybe I was wrong.'

Roberts stared into the big Lakota's eyes, then stuck out his hand.

'I appreciate it, White Elk. I know you don't do half the things everyone says. Stay out of trouble and stay away from the Big A. Appleton won't take this too kindly. I expect we're in for trouble.'

White Elk nodded and walked away.

Roberts turned and headed back towards the office. He needed to find Deputy Leggot and tell him what happened. He figured it would be wise to get ready for when Appleton found out what happened.

Roberts didn't have long to look as Leggot ran up from behind the hotel.

'I heard you killed Frank Gerard. It's all over town and it looks like we're in for it now. The old man isn't going to sit still and let someone kill his foreman even if it was self-defense.'

Roberts looked down at his deputy – who, at five foot ten, was four inches shorter.

'I knew there'd come a day when Frank's big mouth would do him in,' he replied. 'He would have dropped White Elk right on the spot if I'd let him. I couldn't believe he missed.' He paused, then added: 'Come to think about it, even if he had plugged White Elk, I'll bet the big man would have gone down with his hands around Frank's throat.'

Roberts took his hat off and wiped the

inside sweat band. 'I'm not looking forward to riding out to the Big A and telling the old man. He'll take it pretty hard. Frank's worked for him quite a few years.'

'You're probably right, Rush. But they know you can handle yourself. I've never seen a man, white or red, better with a hand-gun than you. Not only that, but I've seen the way you handle a Winchester.'

Shielding his eyes from the afternoon sun, the deputy went on: 'Besides I can help. I could pick up a few boys to give us a little support. That might keep the Appletons from causing trouble.'

Rush shook his head.

'No, I can't see anyone else getting hurt. Besides I need you to stay and keep an eye on things while I'm gone.'

He pulled the dark-blue Colt handgun from its well-oiled holster, broke it open and slipped out the spent cartridge. He replaced it with one from his belt, snapped the cylinder shut with a sharp click, and placed it back into the holster. He didn't like to kill, but if it meant upholding the law, then it had to be done. All the same, it wasn't the type of thing a man got used to.

2

The two lawmen were standing quietly on the sidewalk in front of Jay's emporium when they glanced up the street and saw a beautiful brown-haired woman struggling with three saddle tramps. She was upset and the more she attempted to break out of their grasp, the more they laughed and tormented her.

Both lawmen hurried down the sidewalk. As they approached one of the foul-smelling saddle tramps tried to kiss the woman on the mouth. She tore away from his grasp, slapped his face and screamed for him to leave her alone. Roberts, his face hot with anger, quickened his pace.

Rush seized the nearest saddle tramp, a heavy-set man with a pockmarked face, by the shirt and threw him roughly to the ground. The man jumped up and threw a punch in Roberts's direction. The sheriff neatly sidestepped the attack, then pounded the man with a short right hook, flush on the jaw. The saddle tramp dropped like a sack of wet potatoes. Roberts looked coldly at the other two men.

'You better get out of here,' he barked.

The two cowboys glanced at each other. The uglier of the two snorted.

'Make us, lawman.'

He swung a fist and caught Roberts square in the face.

The force of the blow staggered Roberts and he fell to one knee, his head spinning. Deputy Leggot jumped in and bashed the saddle tramp solidly in the mouth; teeth and blood spurted across the sidewalk. The other man rushed the deputy and threw a tremendous punch at his head. Leggot ducked the blow, then delivered a vicious hit to the saddle tramp's kidneys.

A group of people quickly formed to watch the fight. The attractive brunette, her eyes full of fear, looked at the people standing in a circle around the struggling men.

'Why don't you help them?' she shouted. 'What's wrong with you?'

Tug Jackson, a teamster, looked at her and grinned.

'Don't worry, lady; they can handle themselves, wait and see.'

By then Roberts was back on his feet. He quickly smashed one of the saddle tramps a hard blow to the solar plexus, then followed it up with a tremendous shot to the head. The man folded up like an unstaked tent in a prairie wind and lay crumpled on the sidewalk.

While the deputy and the other cowboy went at it blow for blow, the first man Roberts had laid out jumped on the sheriff's back and tried to gouge his eyes. Roberts grabbed the man's arm and flipped him into the dusty street. Before the cowboy could regain his feet, Roberts rushed in and hit him so hard the sound carried for two blocks. The saddle tramp landed smack-dab in a pile of fresh horse-dung.

Leggot timed an uppercut perfectly and with all his might landed the blow under his assailant's chin. The punch lifted the poor saddle tramp two inches off the ground and sent him sprawling into a nearby barrel holding wooden ax-handles. The fight over, Roberts walked over to a wooden horse-trough and plunged his head deep into the cool water. He stood up and let the water cascade down the front of his shirt. He turned to his deputy.

'You all right?' he asked.

Leggot grinned while at the same time wiggling a loose tooth. 'Never better,' he replied. 'It's been a while since we had this much fun.'

Roberts noticed that the cowboys were regaining their senses, so he approached the ringleader, who was up on one knee shaking the cobwebs from his head. Roberts looked down at the man.

'You've had enough, mister,' he said, 'It's time you and your friends leave Chadron.'

The cowboy looked up and through swollen and bleeding lips mumbled:

'Anything you say, Sheriff.'

'Good. Take your friends and get out of town. If I ever see you again there'll be hell to pay. I'm sure you get my meaning, right, pardner?'

The cowboy nodded his head and stumbled up the street with his friends. Together they walked to Moss's livery stable. They saddled up and rode out of town headed south towards the Platte River Valley, no doubt wishing they'd never come to Chadron.

Rush turned and looked at the lady. She was a tall woman, yet shapely in all the right places, with a crown of soft brown curls cascading down across her shoulders. She carried herself erect and proud, but was visibly angry from what had happened. Her brown eyes flashed and her cheeks were flushed.

'Is this a common occurrence in Chadron, a woman being accosted by thugs?' she accused. 'I would presume as sheriff you would have things more under control.'

The tall lawman flushed with embarrassment from the barb, but remained under control. In fact, it was hard to get mad at someone so beautiful. The smell of perfume filled the air and he noticed her soft, cream-like complexion. He also noticed she was dressed for horseback riding. She wore high, black-leather boots, riding-skirt, and a ruffled white shirt.

'Things happen, ma'am. We just have to deal with them when they come up,' he said.

Looking into her dark-brown eyes, he continued: 'Brad and I figured you needed help so we came running. Isn't that right, Brad? They had no call treating a lady like that and I will not allow it in my town. By the way, I don't think we've met.'

The woman calmed down, grateful to have the help. She did not expect to be accosted in broad daylight and it shook her.

'I guess that's true. My name is Amy, Amy Appleton. And your name is...?'

Roberts cleared his throat and replied:

'The name's Rush Roberts.'

She observed the lawman's strong shoulders, his narrow hips and muscular frame. Although still shaken and angry, she was drawn to his dark, almost black eyes which shone fiercely in the bright daylight. His face was intense, yet not intimidating, exuding a quality of trust and strength she thought admirable.

'Your deputy's name is Leggot, I understood you to say?'

Brad jumped on the sidewalk. He bowed from the waist.

'Deputy Bradley J. Leggot at your service, ma'am,' he piped up. 'Defender of lovely women and small children.'

She couldn't help but giggle at Leggot's comment.

Roberts, pleased with her response, asked:

'Forgive me, Miss Appleton but it appears you might be related to Jake Appleton. He's a big man around these parts.'

'That's right, Sheriff Roberts. You see Jake Appleton's my uncle,' she replied with a warm smile. 'I've been living in Indiana, near Bloomington, but after Father died this spring I decided to come and visit Uncle Jake. My father and Jake were especially close as children, but as time went on it became increasingly difficult for our families to get together. Besides, I thought it was a great excuse to see the West and well, here I am. In fact, I just finished changing clothes and was waiting to ride out to Uncle Jake's when I was attacked by those terrible bullies.'

Not waiting for the lawman to reply, she continued: 'I understand Uncle Jake has a large ranch somewhere close to Chadron, but I'm not sure where.'

Roberts and Miss Appleton looked at each other for several moments, only the sounds of Svenson pounding horseshoes down the street breaking the silence.

Eventually Rush replied.

'Miss Amy, just a little to the north-west of here, your Uncle Jake owns ten thousand acres of the best grazing land in the territory. Not only that, but his cattle are known from here to Chicago. I've known Jake for about five years and never met a finer man unless crossed, then look out. He's meaner than a cornered bobcat.'

A grin spread across Deputy Leggot's face as he changed the subject.

'I'm sure the sheriff would be happy to escort you out to the ranch. Right, Rush?'

Embarrassed by Leggot's offer, Roberts declared:

'Be quiet, Brad. I'm sure the lady has someone more suited to escort her than me.'

'As a matter of fact,' Amy replied, 'I understand my cousin Charlie Appleton is supposed to come in and escort me. I telegraphed Uncle Jake from Big Springs and said I would be arriving today.'

Rush smiled awkwardly while Brad did his best to keep a straight face. It had been some time since Rush was caught at a loss for words and the deputy enjoyed every minute of his friend's embarrassment.

Amy looked at Rush and his heart quickened. He hadn't had this feeling since he'd met his wife, deceased fifteen years before. It was a good feeling but at the same time he knew she wouldn't be interested in a man like himself. She was from the East, educated and a lady of social standing. He was just a two-bit sheriff living from day to day. Besides, she was white and he was red. Around these parts that was enough.

Roberts glanced down the street and watched Charlie Appleton canter his roan pony up to the sidewalk where they stood talking. Recognizing the sheriff standing in front of the hotel, Charlie stopped, dismounted and tied the foam-covered horse to the nearest hitching-post. Roberts noticed the tired horse. It was just like Charlie to ride a good horse into the ground, Roberts thought to himself.

Rush studied the eldest Appleton. What Charlie lacked in height he made up in girth, built something in the order of a brick jailhouse. The weight he packed was solid as a rock and his hands were like huge, hairy paws. His head was shaped like a bullet and he had lifeless grey eyes in between rolls of flesh.

'Just my luck, running into you today,' Charlie sneered. 'Don't you have anything better to do than stand around and talk?'

Roberts's black eyes bore into the rancher's pockmarked face.

'Things haven't changed much since the last time I saw you, Charlie. You still got a smart mouth. By the way, I'd appreciate it if you'd stop at Clay's on your way out of town.'

'What for? I got no business there,' Charlie barked.

His eyes swept the sidewalk in front of him, stopping at the attractive brunette standing behind the lawman.

Roberts cleared his throat, and in a voice edged with tension said:

'I had to kill Frank Gerard not more than

a half-hour ago. Mr Clay's fixing him up right now and someone will need to pay the bill.'

Charlie stiffened and his face grew red with suppressed anger.

'What happened, Sheriff? What'd you do, back-shoot him?'

Roberts ignored the insult.

'He came after White Elk with that big hog-leg he carried,' he replied calmly. 'Accused him of killing and butchering some Big A steers a few nights ago. He didn't give me any choice.'

Charlie's hand slowly inched its way down to the gun-belt slung low on his hip and tied down around his thigh with a thin piece of rawhide. His face was ugly and tight.

Roberts watched the rancher's movement.

'I don't think that's a good idea,' he said, in a slow, measured voice. At the same time he lowered his hand down to his gun-belt and unsnapped the leather thong snugged over his revolver.

Charlie hesitated, his eyes searching for signs of weakness in the lawman's face. Sweat rolled down Charlie's face, leaving a large dark spot on the front of his shirt. Slowly, he brought his hand back up until it rested by his side.

24

'Well, Sheriff, you put yourself in a bad spot. Pa's not going like you killing his foreman. No sir, I don' suppose he'll like it one bit.'

The tall lawman took his hat off and wiped the sweat off his brow, then ran his hand through his thick, black hair.

'I didn't figure he'd jump for joy neither, but what's done is done. I plan on riding out and telling the old man as soon as I can. By the way, Charlie, I want you to meet your cousin from Indiana, Miss Amy Appleton. She had a little problem with some saddle tramps but we got that all settled.'

Charlie turned to the young woman, his eyes looking up and down her firm body.

'Glad to meet you, Miss Amy. We got the telegram yesterday and Pa told me to ride in and pick you up.'

'I can see that, Mr Appleton. I also see your lack of good manners,' she replied icily.

He ignored the intended insult.

'Call me Charlie; we are cousins, you know.'

'I guess we better leave for the ranch, Mr Appleton,' said Amy. 'Uncle Jake's no doubt expecting me and we shouldn't keep him waiting.' She stuck out her hand for Rush to shake. 'Perhaps we'll see each other again.

25

You could come out to the Big A when all this trouble is over. I'm sure Uncle Jake wouldn't mind.'

Rush shook her hand.

'I sure do appreciate the offer, Miss Amy, but I don't know if it's such a good idea, what with me shooting his foreman and all. Besides, I heard he doesn't care much for Indians.'

Amy's face clouded with disappointment, but brightened almost immediately.

'I'm sure I'll get back to town soon and maybe I'll see you then.'

'Maybe,' Rush replied.

The young woman walked across the street, mounted her horse and rode off, Charlie close at her side. They stopped at Clay's funeral home long enough for Charlie to pay the burial bill. Rush watched silently until they reached the end of Main Street and turned out of sight.

He stood and gazed for several minutes, breathing in the last whiffs of her sweet perfume hanging in the summer air. His daydreaming was interrupted when Deputy Leggot slapped him on the shoulder and laughed.

'Rush, put those eyeballs back in their sockets.'

'Mind your own business, Deputy,' Roberts growled.

'Well, well. It seems we got ourselves a case of love at first sight.' Leggot laughed. 'I've heard about it, but never seen it. Sheriff, I think you're in big trouble.'

'Huh?' Roberts grunted. His mind was a thousand miles away. Then the big Pawnee turned and walked down the street towards his office. 'I told you to mind your own business. Don't you have anything better to do than pester me?'

Leggot chuckled and watched his friend walk down the street. Yeah, he had it bad all right.

3

Sheriff Roberts's expression changed to one of concern as he and his deputy neared the office. Two local cattle ranchers, Ben Kingsley and Tom Walker were waiting for them, and by the worried look on their faces, it was evident they had something important on their minds. Roberts knew the two men to be honest, hardworking cattlemen. They had adjoining spreads north-east of Appleton's Big A Ranch, sharing water rights to the clear, fresh streams that ran through the Pine Ridge Valley.

The men offered their hands to the sheriff who shook them one at a time.

'Howdy boys, you look as though you've got a problem. What can I do for you?'

Kingsley, a balding, bow-legged man about fifty years old spoke first.

'I'm going to get right to the point. Sheriff Roberts, someone's rustling our cattle.'

Roberts pursed his lips tightly together.

'Rustling? Are you sure?'

'I don't have any other explanation for it.' Before he could say another word the other rancher stood up and cut him off. Tom Walker was visibly agitated and almost shouted at the two lawmen.

'It can't be anything else but rustling and it's got to stop. We've each lost another ten cows. Not only that, but I know who the rustlers are and if you don't do something about it, I will!' he threatened.

Roberts held his temper. 'Try to calm down and tell me the whole story from the beginning, Mr Walker,' he said. 'But before you get started, let's go inside and get out of the sun.'

28

Deputy Leggot opened the door and motioned for the ranchers to go in. Before following them through the door the two lawmen exchanged glances.

'It looks like we've got a real problem here,' Roberts whispered. 'First the Big A, and now these two; we better get right on it before it gets worse.'

Leggot nodded in agreement as he followed Roberts into the office.

The two ranchers pulled up chairs while Roberts sat down on the edge of his desk, facing them. He looked at them for a long moment then spoke.

'When did you first notice the missing cattle, Mr Walker?'

The angry rancher cleared his throat then replied.

'It was a week ago when one of my men riding nighthawk along Sappa Creek thought he heard noises coming from a ravine. He said it sounded like horses and muffled talking, but since it was pitch-black and he was by himself, he decided to go get help. By the time they got back, no one was there.'

He paused for a moment and then continued: 'Anyway, the next day we happened to be doing a nose-count and come up short eight steers. Naturally we were concerned about the loss and figured they got separated from the main bunch. We sent out a couple of riders to find them, but they didn't see a thing, not one solitary steer. I saw Ben the next day and come to find out the same thing happened to him.'

Roberts got up and walked around his desk.

'Any of your boys notice anything else strange or out of place on the range lately?'

Walker shook his head.

'Not really,' he said. 'We can't figure it out, Sheriff. You would think if those steers were being rustled, we'd find some kind of sign, but we haven't seen anything. It's almost like they disappeared into thin air, excepting the two I found today.'

Roberts looked at the rancher.

'What two are those, Mr Walker?'

'I found two steers stuck full of arrows not more than a mile from the home place early this morning. Sheriff, I've lived here long enough to know what a Sioux arrow looks like and those cows were full of them. It has to be those Indians up on the Pine Ridge. They must not care who knows, leaving those cows like that. Those good-for-nothings, stealing our cattle in the middle of the night and who knows what else! I figure it's

30

White Elk's Cut Off band.'

Ben Kingsley shook his head and frowned.

'Now, Tom. Hold on a minute; we need to let the sheriff here do his job, don't we.' He continued: 'I've gotten to know quite a few of those Cut Offs over the years and if you give them half a chance they'll treat you right. I'm not convinced they're the ones doing it.'

'That's all well and good, Ben, but how do you explain the arrows?'

Kingsley shrugged his shoulders, a look of resignation on his face.

Rush Roberts shook his head and frowned.

'I suppose it could be Indians doing the rustling, Tom. On the other hand I can't say why. I don't think the beef issue's been short lately and besides that, White Elk assured me it wasn't them. It doesn't make sense to leave them arrows for all to see.'

Tom Walker slammed his fist down on the corner of Roberts's desk, sending a pile of papers flying in all directions.

'You're going to believe an Indian over a white man?' he shouted. 'I can't believe what I'm hearing! I'm telling you it was those who done it and if you won't do your job, then maybe I'll do it for you! What's the matter with you, anyway? Afraid to arrest your own people?'

The tall lawman stood up and confronted the angry rancher. He talked slowly, measuring each word.

'I'm going to forget what you just said because I figure you're upset right now and don't know what you're saying.' The lawman's dark eyes flashed and his face tightened. 'By the way you're right I am an Indian, a full-blooded Ki-ke-hakl Pawnee. I fought the Sioux and Cheyenne for thirteen years so people like you and Mr Kingsley could run cattle without worrying about losing your scalps, so don't give me any more trouble about arresting Indians. I'll uphold the law no matter who the guilty parties are. Do you understand me?'

Walker stood nose to nose with the lawman. Eventually he nodded his head and backed off.

Roberts asked the two men where the stolen cattle were last seen. They showed him on a map hanging on the wall behind his desk.

Roberts thanked them and assured them he would investigate immediately. He and Leggot watched as the ranchers walked out of the office, mounted their horses and galloped away.

Deputy Leggot turned and asked:

'What do you think, Rush? I can't figure the Cut Offs to be the ones. I've been up on the reservation more than once and never had any trouble. Sure, I know White Elk gets out of hand every once in a while, but he ain't never hurt anyone. Besides, I don't figure him or the Cut Offs for thieves.'

Roberts shook his head.

'I feel the same way you do, Brad. It just doesn't add up. Why would the Cut Offs leave their arrows sticking in the cattle for us to find? That's just plain dumb if you ask me. Not only that, but I've never known an Indian who can be heard in the middle of the night like the ones the nighthawk supposedly heard in the ravine.'

He shook his head, adding: 'No, I have the feeling that something else is going on here. Trouble is, I haven't got the foggiest idea what. But I'll find out – and I'll find the missing cattle too.'

'I sure hope you're right, Rush,' Leggot replied. 'If we don't find out fairly quickly, I'm afraid we'll have vigilante problems and we don't want that.'

4

Sheriff Roberts felt uneasy as he rode westward out of town. He dreaded the confrontation with Appleton, knowing all about the rancher's hair-trigger temper. He knew it would be hard for Appleton to get over his foreman's death, a man who'd been with him for twenty years.

On the way out of town he passed Moss's livery stable and across the street spotted Clint Harvey, owner of Harvey's Mercantile and Harvey's Last Dollar saloon, among several other Chadron establishments. He noticed Harvey having an animate conversation with a short heavy-set man whom the sheriff didn't recognize as he passed down the road.

Rush knew the Clint Harveys of the world from his days drifting around in Kansas and Nebraska. Gifted with intelligence and a facility for making money, men like Harvey worked hard and soon ended up owning whole towns. Harvey had lived in Chadron for the last fifteen years and owned pretty much every business up and down Front Street. He was no doubt the wealthiest man in these parts, maybe even the entire state.

Harvey's gaze met the sheriffs. He took off his hat and tipped it in Roberts's direction. Rush waved back, recalling a conversation he had with him a few days before. The businessman had explained about how Chadron was progressing towards being a civilized place to live. He made it plain to Roberts that it was his responsibility to clean up the town and make it safe for decent folks to settle and raise families.

After watching Roberts gallop out of sight, the heavy-set man standing beside Harvey. asked:

'Who was that?'

'Sheriff Rush Roberts,' answered Harvey. 'He's as tough as they come, and I'm giving you fair warning, don't even think about messing with him.'

Gil Tomjack's face tightened and his eyes narrowed. He pulled the makings for a cigarette from his pocket and carefully rolled a smoke; then he took a match, flared it on his thumbnail and lit up.

'So that's Rush Roberts the famous lawman,' he declared, exhaling a lungful of smoke.

Hocking up a mouthful of sputum, he spat on the sidewalk and added: 'Hell, he's nothing but a damn Indian.'

Harvey shook his head.

'You may think he's nothing to worry about, Gil, but don't underestimate him. I've seen him in action and there's nobody in these parts that holds a candle to him in pistol or rifle shooting. That includes you.'

The smaller man continued to stare in the direction of the lawman.

'We'll see, I reckon. By the way, you were saying...'

'Oh, yes,' Harvey agreed, nodding. 'You tell Estes and Black Knife that I want more cattle. I need to gear up production. Those Eastern markets can't wait to get more beef.'

'How many do you want? We can get all you can handle,' Tomjack said confidently.

Harvey smiled. He had never dreamed that this scheme would work out so well. There were thousands of cattle in the Pine Ridge Valley for the taking and he wanted them.

'Have them bring in another five hundred. That ought to do for now.'

'Five hundred sounds fine to me, but let's get a few things straight just so I know where I stand. I'm the middleman, right?

You pay me to make sure Estes and Black Knife get the cattle and deliver them to the hideout so their brands can be altered. Right?' Tomjack asked.

'Yes, that's right,' the tall man replied. 'I depend on you to get them the word. I don't want either one anywhere close to town. By the way, I have other ideas for making money besides this cattle operation. I hope you'll feel like sticking around when we're done. I can use a man of your talents.'

Tomjack nodded his head.

'OK, but let's just stick with this operation for now.'

'Sure,' Harvey agreed. Turning slightly, he looked up and down the street, then turned back to Tomjack.

'Let's go inside to my office,' he suggested. 'I don't want anyone to see us together.'

The two men stepped inside the store, walked to the back of the building and entered Harvey's office. Tomjack whistled softly. His eyes took in the plush office interior.

'Pretty nice, Harvey. I'd say business is good, real good.'

Harvey smiled, eager to show off his wealth to the gunfighter. He sat down and pointed to an overstuffed chair.

'Sit down, Gil.'

Tomjack moved slowly through the office, taking it all in. The walls of the office were decorated with large stuffed game-heads which Harvey had acquired over years of hunting in the North-west. The thick carpet was a dark blue, and the huge, polished-oak desk sat in one corner, papers strewn across its surface. Several brass lamps sat on expensive wooden tables, and next to the desk was a well-stocked liquor cabinet. Tomjack's eyes immediately went to the half-filled bottles of amber-colored liquor, his tongue licking his thick lips in anticipation.

Harvey noticed the man's interest in his whiskey.

'Would you care for a drink?' he asked. 'I don't mind saying I've got the best Irish whiskey between Omaha and Denver,' he added holding up a beautiful cut-glass whiskey-decanter.

'Don't mind if I do, Mr Harvey,' Tomjack replied. 'I'd take about three fingers.'

The taller man got up, poured a generous portion into a crystal whiskey-glass and gave it to the cowboy. He eased into a chair facing Tomjack.

'Are you sure you can trust this Estes and that Indian, Black Knife?' he asked.

38

'I'm as sure as I can be,' Tomjack replied.
'You never really know, but I think so. You
keep paying Estes and giving the Indian
whiskey and I don't think we'll have any
problems.'

Just as Harvey was about to reply, there
was a knock on the office door. He walked
over to the door and opened it. A dirty,
unshaven, man wearing a tied-down holster
stood at the doorway. Harvey eyed the man
suspiciously.

'What can I do for you?' he asked.

Gil Tomjack recognized the shadowy
figure. He rose and walked up behind Harvey.

'Mr Harvey, this here's Steve Estes.'

Tomjack turned to the stranger leaning
against the doorway. 'What the hell are you
doing here?' he asked angrily. 'I told you
never to come into town, especially in broad
daylight. Have you gone loco?'

Estes lounged in the doorway staring at
the two men.

'Yeah, yeah you told me. The only thing is
that sometimes I don't listen very well. You
got a problem with that?'

Tomjack stiffened and a cruel glint came
into his eyes. He didn't like Estes and would
like nothing better than to teach him some

39

manners. Because the man was doing a good job with the cattle, he let the remark go unchallenged.

'I just don't think it's a good idea and I don't think Mr Harvey does either,' he snapped, nodding to the tall man standing beside him.

Up to this point Harvey had never met Estes. He looked the man over. 'Tomjack's right, you shouldn't have come here,' he said. 'What if someone should see us together? We don't want to blow this operation.'

Harvey hurriedly ushered the dirty gunman into the office then looked down the hallway to see if anyone was watching. Satisfied that no one had paid any attention, he shut the door. When they were all seated Harvey stared at Estes.

'I don't want you coming here,' he declared, 'but now that you're here, let's talk about the job. How's it going? Are you having any trouble with the local ranchers?'

Estes pulled a ready-made cigarette from a vest pocket and fumbled through his pants pockets for a match.

'No trouble, no trouble at all,' he replied. 'Me and Black Knife's been working the south range over pretty good and those dumb ranchers still don't know what's going

40

on. Using unshod ponies just like the Indians was a great idea.'

Having found the match, he struck it against one of Harvey's expensive wooden chairs, then lit the cigarette and blew smoke directly into the businessman's face.

Harvey coughed from the cigarette smoke, then cleared his throat.

'I'm glad to hear it, Estes,' he said. 'I take it nobody's been hurt so far either.' He paused for a moment then continued: 'I don't want anyone hurt, but you know what to do in the event that you get caught, right? This operation is far too big to be stopped by some nosy rancher.'

Estes smiled, then reached down and patted his gun.

'Nothing I enjoy more than taking care of little problems like that, Mr Harvey.'

Tomjack got up and walked over to Harvey's desk. He sat on the corner. He took his pistol out of the leather holster and nonchalantly spun the cylinder. He liked the clicking sound it made and the cool feel of gun-metal on his skin. He looked up.

'Say Estes, I was wondering if you knew who the sheriff was in this town?' he asked.

'Naw, I don't know and I don't care. Who-ever he is, I'll bet he's stupid. Most of these local sheriffs are pushovers.' Estes's eyes narrowed suspiciously. 'Why?'

Tomjack chuckled softly.

'Maybe it's no big deal, but I happen to know his name,' he replied. 'You ever heard of a man named Rush Roberts?'

Estes straightened up immediately, his dark features clouding in anger.

'Roberts! Here?'

'It seems I struck a nerve.' Tomjack replied. Scratching his head, he continued: 'Wait a minute … yeah, I remember now, weren't you and him mixed up in those killings down on the Republican River some years back?'

Estes was visibly angered.

'Yeah, he was there along with all those mangy Pawnee friends of his. We caught them by surprise down on the Republican in a box canyon. Black Knife and I did a job on them. They shouldn't have been in Sioux territory hunting buffalo. It's too bad we missed Roberts.'

'It's funny how time changes things, Estes. I heard you and your Sioux friends killed about a hundred Pawnee women and children, but not too many warriors,' Tomjack countered.

The gunfighter stood up and confronted Tomjack.

'You calling me a coward?' he growled. 'I didn't know you were such an Indian-lover.'

'Settle down, both of you,' Harvey barked. 'We got more important things to do than dredge up the past and call each other names, so sit down and shut up!'

Both men glared at each other. Then reluctantly each sat down.

'How long will it take you to get five hundred head of cattle? Harvey asked.

'Five hundred ... I figure no more than a week,' answered Estes. 'Make sure you have the men down at the hideout ready to go a week from today and you'll see plenty of cows. Can you get enough men to drive them up to the railroad station at Niobrara?'

Harvey and Tomjack nodded in agreement, then Harvey said:

'That won't be a problem; just make sure you get the cattle where they're supposed to be.'

Before Estes could respond, Tomjack told him firmly:

'If you're wondering about the money, it's just like last time. You'll get it in gold when the job is done. That seemed to work satisfactorily the last time.'

Estes shifted nervously in the chair and crushed out his cigarette. He nodded. 'Yeah,

OK. But we get the full price as long as there are five hundred cattle there, right?'

'That's correct,' Harvey wearily agreed. 'I think we're all set. Are there any more questions?'

Estes walked over to the door.

'No questions.'

Harvey stood up and motioned towards the back room.

'Leave by the back way. It pays to be careful in this business, don't you agree?'

Estes glared for a moment at the taller man, then nodded his head.

'Whatever you say, Harvey.' Then he walked across the office and out through a door leading to the alley. Tomjack got up and followed Estes, careful not to let anyone see him come out from the alley onto the street.

Harvey closed the door behind them. Sighing with relief, he walked back to the liquor cabinet, poured himself a drink, and sat down. He took a sip, then reached into a humidor and pulled out an expensive Cuban cigar.

He felt pretty good about how things were progressing. Not only was he the wealthiest man in the territory, but he would soon be even richer. Using Black Knife and Estes to

44

rustle the steers and take them to the hidden stronghold was smart. Having Tomjack alter the brands, and moving them up to Niobrara for shipment back East was a stroke of genius.

The best part of the plan was throwing off everyone by leaving a few unshod hoof-prints and some cattle shot full of arrows. The sheriff had to think it was the Sioux on the Pine Ridge reservation doing the rustling. Nobody trusted the Indians any-way, so why not blame them? He took a long puff on the cigar and said out loud:

'Why not indeed?'

5

The Pine Ridge Indian reservation lay twenty miles north-east of Chadron, and another three miles beyond that sat the Big A Ranch. Sheriff Roberts trotted his black stallion along the road leading towards the Indian Reservation, then abruptly changed his mind and decided to cut through a series of draws and hills where some of the cattle had been stolen. If he was lucky, maybe he'd discover some sign leading to the where-abouts of the missing steers.

The sun was well up in the sky and it was getting hot. Roberts tugged his hat lower in front to shield his eyes from the glare, and went on. Near midday the trail began to bend toward several low hills and bluffs covered with emerald-green pine-trees. The smell of the fragrant pine-needles filled the air and, to escape the sun's heat, Roberts headed for the nearest hill. He noticed several spots along the trail that would be perfect places to ambush unwary sheriffs. A well-placed bullet fired from one of these hiding-places and he would be coyote bait.

Reining in, he was ready to dismount when he saw a small creek not more than fifty yards down the hill. Nothing looked better to the dusty and tired lawman than the fast-moving, clear stream shimmering through the trees.

Picking his way carefully down the hill, he suddenly stopped, his eyes snapping down to the ground. He saw what appeared to be horse- and footprints running alongside the narrow trail. Although the ground was dusty from the prolonged heat spell, he could still make out the dusty outlines. He glanced around in every direction then dismounted for a closer look.

Kneeling on one knee, Roberts studied several sets of horse-tracks as well as a pair of footprints. Upon closer examination, he discovered the footprints were made by men wearing moccasins and the horses were clearly unshod ponies. His old tracking days with the Pawnee scouts paid off as he recognized the moccasins by their shape and contour. The lawman slowly stood up, took off his hat and ran his fingers through his sweaty hair. Whistling out loud, he muttered: 'Sioux.'

The tracks ran for another twenty yards until they disappeared, the ground beyond being covered with a soft carpet of pine-needles. Pretty smart, he thought to himself. It was evident that these Indians hadn't forgotten any of their tricks since being 'civilized' by the white man. They did exactly what he would have done if he didn't want anyone following him.

Deciding to rest a little before going on, he walked over to the shade of a nearby pine-tree and loosened the stallion's saddle girth. That done, he sat down and leaned back against the tree, wondering where the Indians went and what they were doing on this land. It wasn't part of the reservation so they would have no need to be traveling across it, yet someone had just passed through.

Suddenly the lawman's eyes caught sight of a thin wisp of smoke trailing skyward over the nearby horizon. It came from beyond a stand of trees further to the north. He studied the slow rising ribbon of smoke carefully. It was too far south to come from the reservation and too far east to come from Kingsley's and Walker's spreads, so he ruled out all those possibilities. His heart quickened. It could be whoever he had just caught sign of, but he doubted they would leave such an obvious signal as to their whereabouts. He decided to check it out.

Roberts stood up and tightened the saddle then mounted and struck off across the stream. Water splashed up and soaked his pant-legs as he spurred the black towards the smoke. After riding up and down several small hills, Roberts entered a deep ravine full of tightly spaced pine-trees, so thick with underbrush it was all he could do to just get through. Cursing the branches clutching at his clothes and horse, he eventually burst out of the entanglement into a small, open park.

He should have come out close to the fire,

but he'd lost sight of the smoke as he came through the underbrush. Dismounting, he slowly drew the Colt .45 from its holster. Leaving the stallion tied loosely to a willow-bush, he continued on across the small stretch of open ground covered with long-stem goldenrod and colorful wildflowers. Stepping quickly, he entered another thick patch of underbrush.

He stopped and peered into the tangled brush, listening closely. He looked for movement, or a sign, but saw nothing. Then, the sound of a horse nickering floated down through the underbrush. His stallion whinnied in response.

Cautiously, Roberts picked his way through the trees, then plunged down a steep slope into a path of tangled undergrowth. Fighting his way through the thick brush, he slowly worked his way down the hill. He was careful and moved like he'd been taught as a young man, keeping his eyes and ears alert for danger.

It happened fast. Before he knew it, Roberts felt the cold steel edge of a large knife across the length of his throat and the iron lock of strong arms pinning his arms tightly to his chest. He struggled to get loose, but it was no use, the man who held him was very powerful. Sweat rolled down the lawman's neck as he struggled against the assailant's iron grip.

Knowing it was useless to resist, he stopped struggling, then heard a voice whisper in his ear.

'It's me – White Elk. If you promise to put your gun away, I'll let you go.'

Relieved that it was White Elk, he nodded his head in agreement. The big Indian let him go and together they walked into a small clearing. Rush turned and looked at White Elk.

'I thought I'd had it for sure back there,' he said, relief flooding his face. 'I saw all my ancestors in the shadow land when you laid that pig-sticker across my throat.'

White Elk threw his head back and laughed.

'You should be ashamed of yourself. And here you are, an Indian, letting me sneak up on you. It must be town living. It's turned you soft like the white man.'

'I guess you're right.' Roberts grinned and looked around. 'What are you doing out here anyway?'

The lawman's smile turned into a scowl as he looked around and spotted a dead steer lying near a clump of willows. Its bloody skin lay draped across a stout dog-cherry bush and was drying in the hot summer breeze. The gut bag lay next to a smoldering fire, while the rest of the cow lay quartered and ready to be moved

White Elk confronted the lawman.

'Sheriff, you've known me a long time and I never done nothing against the law except have a little too much liquor once in a while. I get drunk, you put me in jail. I sleep it off and go home, right?'

The sheriff nodded.

'When were you last on the reservation?' White Elk asked.

Roberts thought for a second.

'It's been a long time. Why? What's happening up there?'

White Elk shook his head.

'You don't know what it's like. My people are hungry. The beef issues are late and when they do come, they're short. My people need to eat now, not three weeks from now. The young ones cry because their stomachs are empty and the old ones die of sickness because they have no broth. Yes, I killed and butchered this cow, but it's one of many the white ranchers have and will not be missed.'

Rush took his hat off and scratched his

head. He didn't like it, not one bit. It was evident White Elk was rustling cattle, but was he the one who was taking all of the rancher's cattle? Could he be stealing them on such a grand scale? Or was White Elk just one of many Indians from the reservation taking the steers?

'You haven't taken more than a couple, have you, White Elk?'

The Indian stared across the clearing for several silent moments. 'My people need the meat, but I only take what I think the white man won't miss,' he replied. 'We're not doing all that rustling, that I can promise.'

Roberts wanted to believe him but the evidence was strong against it. If Jake Appleton or Tom Walker got wind that White Elk was butchering cattle, there would be hell to pay. It would give the ranchers an excuse to go and clean out the entire Pine Ridge reservation. Many people would die.

The lawman looked at White Elk.

'We've still got a problem. Go ahead and finish butchering this steer and get the meat back to the reservation, but don't do it any more,' Roberts ordered.

White Elk's face tightened with anger.

'I'll see what I can do about the beef issue,' Roberts continued. 'I'll talk to the agent and find out what I can. There's no reason for the meat to be short, no reason at all, 'lessen someone's lining their pockets at your expense. In the meantime, stay away from the cattle.'

White Elk stared at the lawman. Maybe he could trust him after all.

'You are right, Rush Roberts. I will take the meat home and not come back to this place.'

'Good,' replied the sheriff.

'But,' warned the Indian, 'If we don't get the beef issue soon, I will tell our young warriors where there are many beef cows and we will take them. We will not care if the white ranchers try to stop us. It is better to die a warrior than starve like a dog. You must know this, Rush Roberts.'

Roberts nodded his head.

'I know,' he said quietly and turned away.

6

Nearly two hours later Sheriff Roberts arrived at the Big A spread, a huge ranch of about 10,000 acres. Riding along a worn path leading to the ranch house, he grew uneasy. He glanced around the ranch yard, his eyes darting from one direction to another. Some fifty or sixty head of cattle grazed in small groups on either side of the path leading to the main house. There was no one in sight.

The lawman reined the big black away from the path and towards a house shadowed by a small bluff and several giant cottonwood trees. A small stream trickled its way behind the house and out into the green valley. Alongside the house were several other wooden buildings, a barn, bunkhouse, kitchen, and what appeared to be a tack house. The wooden buildings were in good repair, but that didn't surprise Roberts. Jake Appleton had the reputation of taking good care of all his possessions. Rush rode up under the trees and swung down

54

from the saddle.

As he dismounted he couldn't help but wonder where everyone was. It was midday and there should have been all kinds of activity going on at a ranch. He stepped onto the porch and knocked at the front door. He heard footsteps coming to the door. Looking around the yard, Rush couldn't help shake the feeling that someone was watching him.

Charlie Appleton opened the door. Recognizing the lawman, he said sarcastically 'Well, well, if it's Sheriff Roberts, come all the way out here just to say hello.'

'This isn't a social visit,' Rush replied. 'I come to see the old man. Is he here?'

'No, there's only me and little brother Bill here today, all the rest are out looking for our missing cattle.' Charlie stared angrily at Roberts, then continued: 'You know, the cattle you're supposed to be finding.'

Rush ignored the insult.

'Do you have any idea when Jake will be back?'

'Not until dark, I reckon. They're checking the ravines on Pine Ridge. The old man thinks the Sioux are to blame.'

Roberts's face tightened with anger.

'I sure wish your pa would let me do the investigating, Charlie. Someone's going to get killed before this is over. By the way, where's Billy. I didn't see him when I came in.'

'I expect he's out in the barn doing chores. What's it to you?' Charlie snorted.

'I guess it doesn't matter, but I've had this feeling someone's been pointing a rifle at my back ever since I got here, and I don't like it.'

The big lawman stepped back off the porch and looked across the open yard. He scanned the yard until his eyes caught sight of the youngest Appleton son standing just inside the barn door aiming a Winchester smack-dab at his belly-button.

Rush took a deep breath and walked slowly over to the barn. He stopped about twenty-five feet away.

'Come on out, Billy,' he said. 'And drop the rifle on your way.'

Billy reluctantly came out from within the shadow of the barn door and glanced at his brother standing just on the porch.

'Is it OK, Charlie?' he yelled. 'I mean, to drop the rifle?'

'Sure, Billy,' Charlie answered. 'The sheriff wants to talk to you.'

'Listen,' said Rush, 'I don't want any trouble, so drop the gun.'

Billy grinned. 'I'll drop it, Sheriff, but you're going have to fight me before you leave. Charlie's been telling me how bad you need a licking. He says I should break your back.'

Rush stared up at Charlie's younger brother. For his age, Billy was the biggest man Rush had ever seen, wide in the shoulder with a massive chest and huge hands. He stood almost six foot five and his body was massive.

'Now, Billy, you don't want to go around breaking people's backs, it's not polite.' Staring at the huge man-child, Rush continued: 'It's been a while since I've seen you. You sure have gotten a lot bigger since the last time I was here.'

Billy set the rifle against the barn door and walked slowly over to the lawman. 'That's right, and Pa says I'm not done growing yet.' Looking over at his brother on the porch, Billy asked: 'Is he bothering you, Charlie?'

Charlie grinned. 'Oh, not really, Billy. It's just that he was telling me how big and stupid you are, and that God didn't give you the sense he give a goose.'

Billy frowned and fixed an angry stare at Roberts.

'Now, just hold on there, Billy. I never said any such thing. I don't want any trouble,' Roberts said, backing away.

Billy rolled up his sleeves.

'I guess it's time you learned a lesson, Sheriff,' he said, 'so take off that gun-belt and get what's coming to you.'

'Forget it, Billy. Can't you see Charlie's just trying to start something? I don't want to hurt you.'

The boy-giant laughed.

'Shut up. I want to enjoy this. I never beat up an Indian before.'

The lawman's eyes narrowed.

'Have it your way, Billy,' he said flatly.

Billy's eyes blinked. He was startled and felt a reluctant admiration for this man. There he was, a big man unchallenged for strength and fighting fury. There weren't too many men around Chadron who would fight him one on one, yet the sheriff was ready to fight.

Rush knew he could place three shots within an inch of Billy's heart if he wanted to, but there wasn't any need for gunplay. He unbuckled his gun-belt and let it slide to the ground.

'I could kill you, Billy,' he said. 'But, instead, I'm just going to teach you a lesson.'

'Is that right?' Billy shot back.

'That's right.' Rush grinned. 'Let's get to it.'

Billy roared, then lunged, but Rush's hands were up and he stabbed a sharp left to the teeth that flattened Billy's lips back. A lesser man would have been stopped in his tracks, but it didn't even slow down young Appleton.

One of Billy's huge fists caught Roberts a jarring blow as he rolled to escape the punch. But with the same roll he threw a right to Appleton's heart. It landed solidly, and flat-footed, feet wide apart, Rush pivoted at the hips and hooked his left to Billy's belly. The punches landed hard and they hurt. Roberts went down in a half-crouch and hooked a wide right that clipped Billy on the side of the head.

Appleton stopped in his tracks and blinked.

'You ... you hit pretty hard!' he stammered, his face full of surprise.

Then he growled and advanced. He punched swiftly, left and right. Rush slipped away from the left, but the right caught him in the chest and knocked him to the ground. Billy rushed him, but Roberts rolled over and came up as Billy closed in. Rush

59

smashed a wicked right to the belly, his fist sinking deep into the young man's paunch. Billy doubled over, clutching his gut in agony, and the sheriff exploded two splintering punches on his chin. Billy shook his head, sucking great gasps of air into his lungs.

Rush couldn't believe it. Nobody had ever taken those punches and kept their feet. He was beginning to get worried.

By now, Billy had his second wind. The young giant punched at Rush's face, the blows thudding against cheek-bone and skull until the lawman wrenched his way free. Seeing an opening, Rush smashed down with the inside of his boot against Appleton's shin, driving his weight on the big man's instep. Billy let go with a yell and staggered back, and then Rush hit him flush on the jaw.

Billy staggered back several feet, his eyes blinking back the pain. Rush stared at him through trickling sweat and blood.

'How'd you like that?'

Billy felt around his mouth with his fingers until he pulled out a big molar. He smiled through bloody lips and threw the tooth at Rush's head.

'Not too bad for a little man!' he yelled,

then smashed a right to Rush's ribs that stabbed pain in his vitals. Rush staggered back and fell, gasping wide-mouthed for air. Billy came in and they stood toe to toe, hitting each other with terrible blows, thrown with wicked power. Billy's face was pulp, a huge bruise was under one eye, almost closing it. There was a cut on Roberts' cheekbone and he could taste the blood as it trickled into his mouth.

Then Rush stepped back suddenly. He caught Billy by the shoulder and pulled him forward, off balance. At the same time, he smashed a right in the man's kidney.

Billy staggered and Rush moved quickly in. He stabbed a wild left to the mouth then another. Then a hard-driven left to the body followed by a right.

Rush circled warily now, staying out of reach of those huge hands, away from that incredible bulk. He was tired, and his arms felt like lead weights. Setting himself for one last tremendous blow, he connected a right to Billy's body. Billy fell back a full step, his head swaying like that of a drunken sailor.

Rush moved in. He set himself and whipped a right to the body again, then a left and another right, each blow strong enough to drop a normal man. At last Billy went down in a heap.

He struggled to his knees and raised his arms in protest.

'Enough. Enough!' Billy said, wiping the blood from his mouth. 'I won't cause you any more trouble, Sheriff. You win.'

Shaking his head, Roberts replied.

'I hope you mean it, boy. It's been a long time since I tangled with anyone the likes of you.'

The lawman reached down, picked up his hat and batted it against his leg. Turning to Charlie, he stared coldly at him. 'I come here to tell Jake I'm doing the best I can about finding the rustlers. Tell him that and this too. I don't want him taking the law into his own hands. Let me handle it. He'll know what I mean. Tell him!'

He turned and headed toward his horse when suddenly he heard footsteps coming from behind. He whirled around and saw Charlie advancing, a pistol in his right hand.

Roberts was lightning-fast. He snapped off a shot that exploded the gun out of Charlie's hand. The oldest Appleton boy howled in pain as he dropped to one knee.

Roberts holstered his gun and walked to where Charlie kneeled, groaning on the ground. Standing over him, he said:

'That was a stupid play. I could have killed you and for what?' He shook his head and continued: 'You were lucky this time. Don't ever try it again.'

Billy helped his brother up. He pulled out a dirty kerchief and wrapped it around Charlie's bleeding wrist.

'Sheriff, I think it's best you move along. Charlie needs some tending. I'll make sure Pa gets the message.'

'Billy, tell your pa I'm sorry I had to kill Gerard. And I'm sorry I winged Charlie. He probably won't understand, but tell him just the same.'

Roberts mounted the stallion and rode away without looking back.

7

Anxious to return before dark, Roberts followed a washout up to a ridge's crest, over a saddle and into a deep pocket in the hills that lay under the east rim of Pine Bluff. Picking up a faint Indian trail, barely discernible for night was coming on, he followed it across the head of White Clay Creek to Dark Canyon.

Darkness on the Pine Ridge brought coolness as a soft evening breeze danced down the canyon. Roberts dismounted and stripped the gear from his horse. He would wait and ride into Chadron tomorrow; besides, the fight between him and Billy Appleton had left him more than a little sore and a solid night's sleep would do him good.

Roberts camped under a shoulder of rock on White Clay Creek, where there was a small space of hard-packed sand and a trickle of water from a freshwater spring. There were no trees, just some low-growing willow and chokecherry, but there was grass further down the hollow where he hobbled the stallion. Gathering an armful of twigs and dry moss he soon had a small fire burning. He walked down to the spring, filled a worn coffee-pot with water and it wasn't long before the smell of freshly made coffee drifted to his nostrils.

He rummaged around in his saddlebags and came out with a handful of deer jerky. Munching on the tough meat, he took out the makings for a cigarette and laid them on the ground next to his saddle.

He poured a cup of steaming coffee,

leaned back against his saddle and stared into the flickering fire. Every time he traveled this country he could see why men fought over it. It had some of the finest grazing land in the world when the season was right. If you had rain, or good winter snows that could melt and sink in, you had grass, and a lot of it.

Cattlemen would do almost anything to protect their land, including lynching anyone they felt guilty of rustling their cattle. He didn't blame Tom Walker, Ben Kingsley, or Jake Appleton for their anger, but on the other hand the law's the law and he was getting paid to uphold it. No man had the right to take the law into his own hands, no matter how right it might seem.

He washed the jerky down with a cup of strong coffee and rolled a cigarette. He lit up, and he inhaled the pungent smoke, his thoughts drifting to the Sioux on the Pine Ridge. He didn't want to believe they were rustling those cattle. Sure, it appeared they were taking a steer or two, but the number disappearing was too many for them to handle. They couldn't butcher that many cows without arousing suspicion. Besides, White Elk said his people weren't doing it. Roberts wanted to believe the Indian but how could he know for sure?

Roberts stubbed out the cigarette on the ground. He realized how tired he was. He checked the hobbles on his horse, then rigged up a cozy place to sleep near the fire. He threw a few more small branches on the flames and lay down, his Winchester close by. It paid to be careful. He was asleep before his head hit the saddle.

The coals glowed a deep red, their light reflecting on the still figure wrapped up in a blanket lying comfortably against the saddle. It was a dark night as a heavy cloud cover obstructed the stars from view. It was quiet, except for the occasional hoot of a horned owl and the mournful cry of a lonesome coyote echoing down the canyon.

Moonlight streaming from a sudden break in the clouds revealed two shadowy figures moving from rock to rock, their moccasined feet not making a sound. Slowly they edged closer and closer to the figure lying near the fire. They quietly approached to within twenty yards, nodded to each other, then fitted arrows to tightly strung bows and with a bloodcurdling yell, rose up and shot directly at the sleeping man.

The arrows zipped through the air, penetrated the blankets, and stuck there quivering from the force of the bows. Rushing the camp, both men laughed while pulling razor-sharp scalping knives. One of the men leaned over and pulled the blankets back. His face registered surprise as the 'dead' man he expected to see was a dummy bedroll. He stood up to tell his friend when a rifle coughed twice from behind a nearby rock.

Earth sprayed in the air as the heavy bullets struck the ground in front of them.

The two assailants stumbled backwards; then regaining their balance, ran for the shadows. The rifle coughed again and a scream filled the night as the slug hit one of the men. He stumbled, regained his balance and ran down the slope.

Roberts cursed as the rifle mechanism jammed. The last shell had ejected improperly and was stuck in the rifle. He threw the weapon on the ground and pulled his Colt. Jumping out from behind a large rock he ran after the fugitives. While he ran clouds covered the moon once again and it was very dark. He could hear the sound of men crashing through the undergrowth but by the time he got down the hill it was too late. They had escaped.

67

Roberts holstered his handgun and walked back to the fire. He looked down at the bedroll he had fixed up to look like a sleeping man and yanked out the arrows buried deep in the blankets. He had always been a light sleeper and when a loud coyote call aroused him during the night, he decided that maybe there was more than a four-legged critter out and about.

He stoked the fire and studied the arrows in the firelight. Sure enough they were Cut Off Sioux. Maybe White Elk was lying after all.

Satisfied that his attackers had high-tailed it down the hill, he lay down and tried to sleep, but it was no use. He had too much on his mind. He would go back to town in the morning and then see if any more cattle had been reported stolen. Then he would see about going up to the reservation.

The sun had just broken over the eastern horizon when Roberts reached the outskirts of Chadron. After the night's excitement he decided to head for town as soon as possible. He had some things to check out and there was no sense waiting.

It was early and the town was quiet. There wasn't a person on the street except for a couple of merchants setting out goods on the sidewalk for the day's business. He rode up to the front of his office, dismounted and walked in. Deputy Leggot stood near the pot-bellied stove and the aroma of fresh coffee filled the room.

'Good to see you, Rush,' the deputy exclaimed. 'I didn't figure you getting in before noon. How'd things go at the Big A?'

Rush wearily pulled up a chair and sat down. He took off his hat and threw it on a nearby desk.

'Not good.'

He proceeded to tell the deputy about running into White Elk, his fight with Billy Appleton, and the almost night ambush. Leggot listened with avid interest, raising his eyebrows when Rush related how someone had tried to kill the lawman while he slept.

When Roberts finished, Leggot laughed.

'You say that Billy Appleton hit pretty hard, huh? I wish I could have been there to see it, the mighty Rush Roberts getting knocked on the seat of his pants, from a youngster at that.'

The smile disappeared from his face as he continued: 'Who were those men, Rush? I reckon whoever's stealing the cattle will feel secure if you were out of the way.'

Rush shook his head.

'I don't know, Brad. But there's one thing I hope, and that's that the Sioux aren't doing it.'

Leggot agreed. 'Me, too, but the ranchers are still figuring they're the ones doing the rustling. We better catch whoever it is quick!'

Roberts was about to comment when Amy Appleton strode through the office door. The sheriff's face brightened, but quickly turned to a frown when he noticed the look on her face.

'You're up early today. What can I do for you, Miss Appleton?' he asked.

Slamming the door shut she stared at the lawman.

'I didn't want to waste time, Sheriff,' she said, in an agitated voice. 'I came to see you about beating up Billy. I saw what an awful beating you gave him. It was disgraceful. You should be chasing rustlers, not beating up defenceless boys.'

Rush ran a hand wearily through his hair.

'Miss Appleton, Billy's about as defense-less as a cornered badger,' he replied. 'He dang near took my head off.'

'Well, I don't know what happened but I

can't help but think you have better things to do than make trouble for my family. I know Charlie can get out of hand, but Billy's another story,' Amy retorted.

'It so happens I came out to talk to your uncle and Billy started the fight. I had no choice. And by the way, I *am* looking for the rustlers. I just haven't gotten a break on the case, but it'll happen sooner or later. Now, if you're done chewing me out, I've got other things to do.'

'Good day, Sheriff Roberts,' Amy replied angrily. She turned abruptly and stalked out of the office.

Roberts shook his head. There was one thing about it. Amy Appleton was a hellfire on wheels when she got mad. He looked at Deputy Leggot, who just smiled.

'What are you smiling about?' Roberts asked.

'Nothing really. I just never saw you take a chewing from a woman before.'

'Shut up,' Roberts barked as he finished his coffee.

Idling away time at the Silver Dollar saloon, Steve Estes was playing poker with Bob Criner and Ed Sharkey, two hardcases who had drifted into town the day before. Neither one was fond of the law, nor did they enjoy listening to Estes boast about how he hated lawmen.

Estes knew he should be out on the range gathering more cattle, but Roberts's being in town was too much for him. He wanted to finish a job started years before and now was his chance. He didn't give a damn what Harvey wanted. Tonight was the night he would kill Roberts.

Estes glanced at the front door while raking in a big pot. A man entered the saloon and stood just inside the batwing doors. At first he was only a silhouette against the outside light, but when he moved away from the door and approached the bar, Estes's face broke into a grim smile. The man was John Cumby, a rancher whom Estes had worked for several months back.

Estes shuffled the cards while he watched the man walk over to the bar and order a beer. He tossed the cards nonchalantly on the green-felt-covered table, pushed his chair back and sauntered over to the bar. In a thick whiskey voice he addressed the bartender.

'Barkeep, give me another shot of Old Anchor and be quick about it.'

He took the glass and turned to face

Cumby. 'Well, well, if it's not John Cumby, owner of the Double B Ranch come to town for a drink. Let me buy you a beer, Cumby. No, wait a minute, maybe it's you who should be buying me one.'

Heads swiveled throughout the bar as patrons eyed the two men. The gunman's voice carried across the smoke-filled saloon, and it grew quiet. Estes repeated in a louder voice:

'I'm talking to you Cumby. Are you deaf or something?'

'Listen, Estes, I didn't come in here to take any guff from the likes of you.' Cumby faced the gunman and continued: 'I fired you because you was stealing from the men. You're damn lucky I didn't tell them or you wouldn't be standing here today.'

Estes stood silently listening to the rancher talk. He raised one arm and waved it in the direction of everyone sitting in the saloon.

'Looks like you're calling me a thief in front of all these folks, Cumby. That's no way to be, is it.' Glancing at Criner and Sharkey, Estes kept shooting his mouth off. 'Isn't that right, boys. Our friend Cumby isn't being too friendly, calling me a thief and all. You heard him call me a thief!'

'That's right, Steve,' Criner parroted back. 'We heard it plain as day!'

Estes turned back towards the rancher.

'You've got a lot of sand, mister, calling me a thief and you not even wearing a gun,' he growled. 'That's not very smart, Cumby ... no, not very smart at all.'

'I don't want any trouble, Estes, and you're right, I don't carry a gun except when I'm hunting varmints.'

'Shut up!' yelled the gunfighter. He motioned to a cowboy standing along the bar. 'Shuck your gun-belt and holster, mister. Cumby's going need it.'

The scared cowboy quickly unbuckled his gun-belt and handed to Estes. The gunfighter took it and threw it at Cumby's feet. The rancher stared down at the gun-belt lying on the floor and was debating whether or not to pick it up, when Deputy Leggot walked through the saloon's front door. Glancing around the room, he quickly sized up the situation. He walked over to Cumby and stepped between the two men.

'What's the problem?' he asked staring directly at the gunfighter. 'We don't like gunplay in this town.'

Estes shifted uneasily, his eyes moving back and forth from Cumby to Leggot.

'This isn't any of your business, Deputy. It's between Cumby and me. If you know what's good for you, you'll keep your nose out of it.'

Leggot ignored the threat.

'You just made it my business, cowboy,' he replied. 'Now, move real easy and take off your gun-belt. We'll go over to the office and work out what's bothering you, but not until you take off the hardware.'

While Leggot watched Estes Criner approached the unsuspecting deputy from behind. He raised his gun and smacked him across the skull, knocking him to the floor. He was out cold. Estes grinned and turned towards Cumby.

Rush Roberts walked slowly toward the Harvey Hotel in the fading light of early evening. He was making rounds when he noticed a crowd gathering on the sidewalk in front of the saloon. There was only one reason for this to happen. Someone was causing trouble and he'd better check it out fast.

Roberts checked the loads in his Colt as he hurried towards the saloon. Shouldering his way through the crowd, he entered the smoke-filled Silver Dollar. Blinking his eyes quickly adjusted to the saloon's dim light.

He scanned the room, slowly gathering in the situation. On the floor next to the piano lay his deputy, unconscious. A man stood along the bar facing Cumby.

Roberts couldn't believe his eyes. Memories of death and sorrow flooded Rush's mind as he stared at the gunman. Here was the man responsible for the cold-blooded murder of his wife and son. Standing in front of him was the man who allowed the murderous Sioux renegade Black Knife to kill almost a hundred innocent Pawnee women and children along the Republican River.

Estes took one look at the sheriff then turned towards the crowd and laughed: 'Look here, if it's not the famous Rush Roberts.' Turning back towards the sheriff he continued: 'It's too bad I didn't finish you off like I did your old lady and brat kid.'

He stopped, then after a few seconds added: 'Hell, it doesn't make any difference one way or the other 'cause you're here and I can finish it right now.'

'I figured we'd meet up again, Estes,' Roberts replied in a hard, flat voice. 'In fact, I was counting on it.' Keeping a wary eye on the gunfighter Roberts turned slightly towards the rancher. 'Back off, Cumby,' he said, 'I'll handle this.'

The frightened rancher took three paces backwards, happy to let the lawman handle the gunfighter. Estes laughed again.

'That's right, Sheriff. I'll kill you first, then the coward standing behind you. I don't mind using the extra shells.'

Calling over to his friends, he barked: 'Criner! Sharkey! After I kill these two, remind me to go over and get a steak at Jordan's. I'll be mighty hungry by then.'

Roberts knew he was dealing with a cold-blooded murderer and had no doubt Estes would do exactly what he promised. The man was mad-dog crazy and it was time someone put a stop to his murderous ways.

The lawman took a deep breath and exhaled slowly, trying to remain calm and keep his nerves steady, but thoughts of the massacre years before flooded his mind. He had tried over the years to blot out the sight of his wife and son lying side by side, dead, but it was impossible. He was glad Estes stood there in front of him!

'There's two ways to do this, Estes. The first is to unbuckle your gun-belt and drop it slowly to the floor. It's against the law to strike a peace officer and threaten folks. The other way is for you to be carried out of here feet first and I hope by God you choose to make a play.'

The gunfighter snorted. 'You really think I'm going to drop my gun like all the other cowards you've faced down, lawman?'

The room was deathly silent.

'No, I don't figure you will,' Roberts replied. 'But that's OK since you're nothing more than a yellow-belly woman-killer who hasn't got the guts to face a man fair and square.'

Roberts spread his feet apart, slowly dropped his hand down so that it hung loosely by his gun, and stared into Estes's face.

'You can draw anytime, Estes.'

Without hesitation Steve Estes snatched for his gun. He was fast, but not fast enough. Rush Roberts's hand was almost invisible as he drew and fired a split second ahead of the gunfighter. Estes's gun roared twice, both bullets splintering the wooden floor in front of the lawman, even as the heavy slug from Roberts's Colt .45 ripped through his chest, exploding the outlaw's heart. Estes was dead before his body hit face first on the sawdust-covered floor.

Roberts swung and covered Estes's two friends. They both were shocked by the lawman's speed on the draw. They stood frozen to the floor.

'Either of you two figure to make a play like him?' the sheriff asked, pointing to the dead man on the floor.

Both men shook their heads.

'Then pick up this piece of trash and get him the hell out of here. Then get out of town.'

While Estes's friends did what they were told, Roberts leaned over the inert form of the deputy and looked him over. He had a lump the size of a goose-egg on the back of his head, but other than that he seemed to be OK. Leggot groaned and his eyes flickered open.

'What happened?'

Roberts grinned. 'You haven't changed a bit. I see you're still not watching your backside. One of Estes's boys cold-cocked you from behind. You've been out for at least five minutes.'

'Help me up, will you, Rush?' the deputy mumbled.

Grabbing him by the arm, Rush picked him up and sat the wobbly deputy down in a nearby chair. Shaking the cobwebs from his head, Leggot saw the blood on the floor.

'Must have been gunplay. Did you kill him?' he asked.

Roberts nodded his head.

'Estes got what was coming to him. I've had a score to settle with him for a long time. It was a matter of time before I caught up with him. That leaves just one more to find and kill.'

John Cumby walked over to the two men and thanked Rush for saving his life.

'Don't worry about it, John. He had it coming from way back.'

Rush, Leggot and Cumby walked out onto the sidewalk. Looking past the rancher, Roberts watched as Amy Appleton walked slowly toward him. Excusing himself from the crowd that had gathered around him, Roberts holstered his gun and went over to meet her.

She stepped close and touched his arm. Looking up at his face, she said:

'I decided to stay in town and see you tonight. I'm sorry for getting so angry today. It's just that all this trouble has everyone on edge and I didn't mean to take it out on you. Can we start over?'

Roberts looked at the beautiful woman.

'That's OK. I know what it means to worry about someone.'

Her concern for him shone in her brown eyes and sent a shiver through the lawman.

'Would you do me a favor?' he asked.

'I'd love to, Sheriff.'

'Call me Rush.'

Her lips curled up into a playful smile. 'Why, I'd be happy to, Rush,' she said, squeezing his strong arm.

Taking Amy by the arm, Sheriff Rush Roberts escorted her down to the hotel for supper. There was no doubt about it; Rush Roberts was falling in love.

8

Clint Harvey stopped in front of Svenson's and slipped down from his horse. He walked in and saw the old blacksmith standing behind an anvil, hammering out a glowing horseshoe.

'Sorry to bother you, but I need some horseshoe-nails. Seems like this damn horse is always throwing a shoe.'

Svenson dunked the horseshoe he was holding with iron tongs in a bucket of water and walked over.

'No problem, Mr Harvey. I think we can handle that.'

'Did you hear about the shooting last night over in the Silver Dollar?' Svenson asked, counting out the nails.

'As a matter of fact I did. It was an unfortunate incident. I hate violence and the thought of someone getting killed in our town makes me shudder,' Harvey replied.

'I agree, but I'm glad we got a sheriff like Roberts who's not afraid to face down these gunslingers. Makes the streets safer. Where are you heading this morning?' Svenson asked.

'I'm just going out for a ride, Ole. Thought I might see the country. The hills are particularly beautiful in the morning. Don't you agree?'

'I guess so,' Svenson declared. 'Keep your eyes peeled. You don't want to run into any rustlers. They seem to be a problem around here these days.'

Harvey stepped into the stirrup and swung up on his horse.

'I'll keep my eyes open, Svenson. You can count on that.'

As Harvey rode north out of Chadron his body stiffened with anger and he shook his head in disgust. Both he and Tomjack had warned the gunfighter to stay out of Chadron and keep his nose clean. This could be a serious problem. Even though he didn't like Estes, the man had been a fair hand with a gun and for the most part had done what he was told. Rotten luck, he thought, and hoped it wasn't a bad omen for things to come.

Heading straight for Pine Ridge, he cut across a series of small ravines and gullies, knowing Tomjack and the rest of the men would be waiting for him in the stronghold tucked deep in the foothills.

The sun was half-way up when Harvey reached several huge cottonwoods that marked the entrance to a blind canyon. Tomjack knew what he was doing when he picked the canyon for the stronghold. Even Harvey, who had been there several times, had a hard time seeing the canyon's entrance. Protected by a series of dense plum-thickets and bushy undergrowth, the entrance was located between two narrow cliffs. The opening was so narrow that no more than one horse could go through at a time. Once a rider was through, the canyon opened to a wide draw flanked on either side by a series of foothills. The ground was covered with sweet grass just right for feeding cattle.

Harvey moved the underbrush away from

in front of the secret entrance and walked his horse through. Careful to put the brush back the same way, he mounted and rode on. He followed a small stream that meandered through the draw until he saw the cedar-log corral.

Harvey stopped and slid down from his saddle. As he dismounted, Gil Tomjack left a circle of four men seated on several stumps and logs. Tomjack looked surprised and grunted to Harvey.

'We were expecting Estes. He should've been back by now.'

Harvey glanced at the men then back at Tomjack.

'He's dead.'

The hard-bitten gunman scratched his four-day growth of whiskers. 'Dead?' he exclaimed. 'I can't believe it. Who did it?'

Harvey frowned. 'The damn fool picked a fight with Roberts's deputy in the saloon last night and did all right until Roberts muscled in. They had a quick draw and Estes got plugged plumb square in the chest. I hear he fell like a sack of potatoes.'

Tomjack poked his hat back on his head, pulled a cigarillo from his shirt pocket and struck a match.

'I knew Roberts was fast, but...' His voice

trailed off to a whisper. He took a lungful of smoke, then let it out and declared: 'What's done is done. He was a damn fool anyway, messing with Roberts in town when he should have been out stealing more cattle. The other two boys must have lost out trying to ambush Roberts then?'

Harvey frowned. 'That's right. They didn't do doodle-squat. I don't know what happened, but I do know they didn't kill Roberts. It seems the Indian trick must have not worked too well. They messed up the ambush and who knows where they got off to. You heard from either one of them?'

Tomjack was silent.

'You don't have any idea, do you? You idiot! What the hell's the matter with you?' snapped Harvey. He wasn't about to let the gunman off the hook so easily. 'I ask you to do a simple thing like get rid of Roberts and look what happened. That snotty gunslinger Estes is lying in Boot Hill and Roberts is still snooping around. Things around here had better change pretty damn quick.' Harvey's eyes narrowed and he continued: 'Do I make myself clear?'

Tomjack straightened up and stared back at the taller man.

'I reckon you don't have to tell me again,

Mr Harvey,' he replied quietly. 'I'll do your dirty work, the killing that is, but back off a little. I don't like being crowded and right now I feel you're pushing a mite too hard.'

Harvey ignored the veiled threat and walked his horse past the men seated around the circle. He studied each of the gunmen. The four men ranged in age from late twenties to early forties. Mostly saddle bums, they lived from day to day, doing other men's dirty work. It was a hard life and the life expectancy wasn't too long.

One of the men, named Luke, stood up. He addressed Harvey.

'Hey, what's going on here? We keep asking your man there,' pointing to Tomjack, 'but he won't tell us a thing. Where are Thomas and Olive? How come they haven't come back yet?'

Harvey took the reins and nudged his horse closer to the wagon. He regarded the man with disdain.

'Unless you're hankering to get your face beaten or worse, keep your trap shut. You're just the hired help around here and don't ever forget it!'

Luke glowered in silence.

Harvey continued: 'I don't know where

those two are and besides that, Estes is down at Clay's funeral parlor all laid out nice and pretty. He got himself killed last night trying to take Rush Roberts. Anything else you want to know?'

Luke's face clouded with anger. He swore at Harvey and took a step in his direction.

'It was your fault he got killed. Roberts is a tough *hombre*. It takes a lot to kill a man like that.'

Luke had taken a step closer to Harvey when Tomjack stepped over to the side of both men. He grabbed Luke's left shoulder and spun him around. Luke's eyes widened as he came face to face with the angry man.

'So you're a tough guy, huh? Let's see how tough,' Tomjack sneered.

Luke shook Tomjack's hand off his shoulder and stood his ground.

'I don't have a quarrel with you, Tomjack.'

Tomjack sucked hard on his cigarillo, making the burning tip glow brightly. Grinning, he planted the tip of the cigarillo firmly against the man's right cheek. Luke screamed and cursed. At the same time his hand went for the Colt stuck in his belt.

'I wouldn't, if I wanted to live to be an old man, Luke,' Tomjack leered.

Luke knew he was in a bad spot, so he let his hand drop away from the gun.

'That's a good boy, Luke. Now you'd better simmer down. The boss man likes co-operation – and means to have it. You threaten him again, and you'll be the one who's sorry. No more lip, understand?'

Luke glared but said nothing and his refusal to answer infuriated Tomjack. The cold-eyed man unleashed a short, stiff punch to the burned cheek, and the man's head snapped back.

'I asked if you understood?' he hissed.

'Yeah,' sputtered Luke as he spit blood on the ground. 'I understand.'

'When you answer me, call me Mister Tomjack,' the gunman growled. 'Now let's hear it.'

Besides the cut lip, which was quickly beginning to swell, the force of Tomjack's blow had made the man's nose start to bleed. He clenched his teeth.

'I understand, *Mister* Tomjack,' he replied.

The gunman glanced at the other men.

'Anybody else want to question the boss?' he snapped.

There was no response. Tomjack gave Luke one more hard look, then leaped into his saddle.

'Let's look at the cattle, Mr Harvey.'

Both men rode away from the stunned circle of men.

The trail, cut in the bottom of the draw, took them around the breast of a hill and brought them to a creek with an open area off to one side. They crossed the shallow creek and moved through a small grove of cottonwoods and at last came out onto the open ground. Clumps of cattle were scattered throughout the meadow, munching the sweet timothy-hay that grew in profusion across the large expanse. A large pole-fence corral stood at one end of the meadow along with several wooden shacks.

Both Harvey and Tomjack were surprised to see Black Knife standing near the corral. Two cowboys sat on the cedar-pole fence behind him and watched intently as they approached. Harvey and Tomjack halted a few feet from the corral.

Harvey gestured toward the cattle.

'You're supposed to be changing the brands on those cattle,' he said loudly. 'What's the problem? If we're going to get these animals back East, we have to make sure they don't show the other brands.'

Pausing for a moment, Harvey glanced at

the two men sitting motionless on the fence, then back at Black Knife. 'Black Knife, I expect an answer.'

Black Knife's greasy long hair hung ragged from under his dirty sweat-stained hat. The Indian stood quietly and grinned wickedly.

'We're taking a break, that is, me and the boys over there,' he said, waving his hand in the direction of the two men by the corral. 'It's awful hot.'

Harvey eyed Black Knife with anger, then said harshly:

'Looks like I'm having all kinds of trouble today. What seems to be the problem?'

'Well, I and the boys think we ought to get more of a cut on the profits, seeing that we're doing most of the work.'

Harvey straightened up in the saddle, then replied: 'I know what I can do. How 'bout you three share in what Estes had coming to him?'

'What do you mean, he had coming to him? What happened?' Black Knife asked.

'Roberts gunned him down last night in the Silver Dollar. He killed him deader than a brain-shot prairie-dog. Oh, I guess you wouldn't have found out yet.'

Black Knife's black eyes burned with anger. He had ridden with Estes for almost fifteen years, drinking and fighting with him the whole way. It didn't seem possible that Roberts was in Chadron, but all the same it suited him just fine. He had unfinished business with the tall Pawnee, business that meant killing.

Harvey continued: 'What do you say, Black Knife? You and your friends want to share Estes's pay?'

Black Knife stared off towards Chadron.

'Never mind the money,' he replied. 'All I want to know is, when I can get my hands on that damn lawman!'

'You must have patience, my fine Indian friend. My plans aren't quite far enough along for us to go off half-cocked. So far we haven't been able to eliminate that sheriff. We'll take our time and grab our chance when it comes along.'

Earlier that day Sheriff Roberts had ridden northwest out of town, stopping at the spot five miles outside of Chadron where he had been bushwhacked and almost killed two nights before. He eased from the saddle and walked carefully over the area. He had checked the ground over the morning before but since the sun had barely been up when he left for town he had decided to check it again in broad daylight.

Returning to the scene of the ambush Roberts once again decided to follow the creek for a short distance. Certain that the would-be killers had ridden into the stream to cover their trail, he checked the creek-banks for miles in both directions, but was unable to see where the riders had left the creek.

Acting on a hunch he headed into a series of cedar-covered bluffs. But coming up empty once again, he reluctantly swung the black around and rode back to Chadron. Something bothered him each time he thought about the Sioux rustling the cattle. It didn't make any sense. Maybe someone else was stealing the cattle and blaming the Sioux, but who?

The setting sun cast long shadows onto Main Street as he rode into Chadron. He was tired and discouraged; he had come up with nothing so far. He decided he'd ride out again the next day. As he approached his office, he saw Ben Kingsley and Tom Walker sitting on the wooden bench under his window. He reined in, slid from the saddle and tied the stallion to the hitching-post. He dreaded the idea of telling the two cattle-men he'd come up empty.

The strain of losing their cattle showed on the faces of the two older men. As Roberts stepped up onto the sidewalk, Walker snorted.

'Well, if it's not the sheriff. Been fishing?'

Roberts's eyes flashed with anger but he kept under control. Kingsley got up and walked over to Roberts.

'Don't pay him any mind, Sheriff. He's just got a lot on his mind, what with all this rustling going on.'

Roberts took his hat off and ran his fingers through his long black hair.

'I know, Mr Kingsley, I know,' he answered glumly. 'I don't suppose you boys heard about the other night yet?'

'What's that, Roberts?'

'Someone tried to bushwhack me in the hills. Unfortunately I never saw who did the shooting and they got away.'

'I knew it!' shouted Walker. 'I bet it was those Sioux from the Pine Ridge. What are you waiting for, Sheriff? Go up there and arrest the whole bunch. You know they're all in it together.'

'Now hold on, Walker. I don't have any proof it was Indians doing the shooting. Just because you think it was Sioux doing the rustling doesn't mean that they're the ones who tried to bushwhack me. I only know one thing. Whoever's doing the rustling thought it best to get rid of me.'

Walker turned around and kicked the wooden bench, splintering one of the legs into two pieces.

Kingsley spoke. 'I apologize for my friend, but we're getting to the end of our rope. In fact the reason we come into town was to let you know that we both lost another twenty-five head each same way as always. They disappear except for one or two we find dead with those damned arrows stuck in their bellies.'

'That's exactly why I don't believe the Sioux are responsible. They wouldn't leave dead cows scattered around with arrows stuck in them. That just doesn't make any sense. Maybe moccasin-sign but not the arrows. It's just too obvious.'

'I don't know who's to blame, but I know the ranchers are getting fed up with it. It won't set good that you were attacked so near the reservation and in the same area where the cattle are being stolen. I'm just saying that something needs to happen and soon. Either that or this whole Pine Ridge is going explode and blood will flow.'

'Mr Kingsley, I think it's time to ride up

and visit the Pine Ridge Agency. I know the finger points to the Indians, but I don't know. God knows, I wish I had a posse of a hundred men to work those hills, but I don't.'

Walker turned around and stared hard at the lawman.

'Believe me, if we need them, we'll have those hundred men you're talking about. The only thing is, we'll use them to clean out the Pine Ridge once and for all, whether you're around to stop us or not.'

Roberts knew the rancher meant what he said.

Jake Appleton stood just outside the kitchen door and surveyed what amounted to his kingdom or domain. He and men just like him had come to this country many years before and wrested the land from the elements. They risked everything in order to be free and have the kind of life they yearned for. Some were ex-drovers who saved up their wages and bought a few cattle. Some had sold everything back East and come to this country to raise cattle. They were men of all kinds, but they had one thing in common and that was courage. It took all the courage a man could muster to fight Indians, drought, blizzards, and floods. They braved wolves, stampedes, tornadoes and rustlers to build their empires and they didn't give up easily when challenged.

Challenged, that was how Jake felt now. It wasn't the number of head that were being rustled. He could stand the small losses. Shoot, he lost more cattle during a two-day blizzard than what had been stolen so far. It was the principle of the thing. Rustlers needed to be caught and strung up as a warning sign to everyone in the valley. It was as simple as that. It had always been that way. To do anything less was a sign of weakness and to be weak meant disaster.

Several minutes later, Charlie came in from doing chores and plopped down on a chair across from his pa.

'I hate to tell you this, but we're missing more stock. I make it about ten head.'

Jake's face turned red from anger and he clenched his fist. Banging the table he cursed.

'God damn it, I can't believe this! Anyone else hit?'

'We lost the ten from the bunch grazing on Pine Creek just south of Tom Walker's place. When I was down there yesterday I ran into Walker and Ben Kingsley. They got hit too same as before. It's the same at each ranch. Cattle gone, and one or two left behind looking like Grandma's pin-cushion.'

Jake shook his head.

'It's those Indians on the Pine Ridge. There isn't any other explanation for it. They come down out of the hills and take what they want. They know the ground like the backs of their hands. I sure wish I could catch 'em in the act.'

Charlie leaned over. 'Amy, how about some of that coffee,' he asked.

Amy walked over and poured her cousin a cup.

'I've been doing some thinking and I think the sheriff's in this up to his eyebrows,' Charlie said. 'He's an Indian and I think he's getting a cut from his friends.'

Amy slammed the coffee-pot on the table.

'You don't know what you're talking about, Charlie Appleton!' she snapped. 'Sheriff Roberts is an honest man. Not only is he trying to find out who's behind the rustling but he almost got killed in a gunfight with that killer Estes. I don't see anyone going out of their way to help him.'

'Now, hold on, Amy,' Jake retorted. 'You have to admit it looks funny, him being an Indian and all. There is nothing more natural than wanting to protect his kind. They stick together, you know. Besides, he killed Gerard ... don't ever forget that.'

'I won't, Uncle Jake, but the way I hear he didn't have a choice. It was self-defense. You can't blame him for wanting to save his own life.'

Jake shook his head. 'Maybe not if that's true,' he said. 'I just don't know.'

He got up and walked out of the kitchen, Charlie trailing after him.

'What's eating you, Pa?' Charlie asked as he followed the rancher out into the sunlit yard.

Jake rolled a smoke and stared out across the open ground.

'It's this rustling thing. We're losing steers and I don't think the sheriff can handle it.'

'You can say that again,' Charlie retorted. 'Why should he? You know he's one of them and won't do anything to turn in his own kind.'

'That may be true but something else is bothering me. I've never known Roberts to do anything to stand in the way of justice. He's got more sand than most and he isn't a coward.'

'You're too soft on him, Pa,' Charlie growled. 'I owe him plenty and just as soon as I can, I'm going set things right,' he added angrily.

'What do you mean?'

'I mean no man does what he done to me and gets away with it. You saw what he did to Billy. Beat him like a dog. He's got it coming.'

'That's no way to talk, Charlie. You may think you're a fair gun-hand but he's out of your class. I've seen Roberts shoot and he's fast.'

Charlie kicked at the ground.

'Don't worry about me. I know how to take care of myself.'

Jake studied his eldest son. He was headstrong and someday he'd pay for it.

'I don't care what happens as long as you stay away from Roberts. You hear me, boy?'

Charlie looked past his father, not wanting to meet his stern look. At last he answered.

'Yeah, I hear you.'

'Good,' Jake replied. 'Now, get my horse. I'm going take a little ride.'

9

Black Knife grabbed the Spencer carbine from its scabbard and checked to make sure the weapon was loaded. He shoved the loading tube full of gleaming brass cartridges back into place and leaned back against the scrub pine-trees next to the loading-pen. Nothing made him feel better than having a loaded rifle in his hands. A red squirrel chattered high in the tree above his head and a soft breeze cooled his sweaty brow. His thoughts turned to Roberts and what had happened six years earlier on the Republican River.

At the time his people, the Lakota Sioux, lived on the Pine Ridge Agency in north-western Nebraska territory. One day in the fall word reached the agency that the Pawnee were traveling from their villages in the eastern part of the territory down to the Republican River valley to hunt buffalo. It didn't take long for him to find enough warriors who would leave the agency in search of the Pawnee. He told the Indian Agent they needed to go and hunt buffalo for the hides and meat. It was a good excuse and the agent was a stupid man. Even though the agent assigned a white man named Gavin to watch after them he knew there was nothing Gavin could do if they decided to hunt Pawnee instead of buffalo once they reached the valley.

They left the agency at night and traveled fast. A week later they entered the river valley in search of buffalo. Once they found the buffalo they would find the Pawnee. On the eighth day they came across a large herd of buffalo feeding near the river. From the top of a nearby hill his eyes searched each ravine and canyon snaking out from the river bottom for sign of their ancestral enemies. The Pawnee were close, he was sure of it. Then he saw them. No warriors but a number of women and children. They were too busy skinning buffalo to see their enemies on the high ground above them.

He waved his rifle in the air and his warriors kicked their ponies into a gallop. War cries split the silence. The Pawnee looked up but it was too late. There was no place to run. Down into the canyon he could see the Pawnee women standing in a circle with arms uplifted, chanting the ancient tribal song – a song of supplication. His warriors plunged down the ravine and drew nearer and nearer. Arrows and bullets flew thick and fast. He shrieked his war cry and knew it would be good. The Pawnee men were too far away to help their loved ones. There would be many scalps taken this day.

A small Pawnee girl, two or three years old, fell from her mother's back and stretched out her arms, begging to be taken with them as more Pawnee streamed past her. But the Sioux offered no mercy and the child was clubbed to death.

Disappointment clouded his face when he spotted a column of white pony-soldiers racing up the valley. The Pawnee survivors poured out of the canyon's mouth and streamed onto the open plain. Now they would be protected by the white soldiers and the killing would stop. He leaped on his horse and signaled for the rest of his men to follow. They rounded up several hundred loose horses and vanished over the hills to the north. It had been a great victory. He turned one last time and watched one Pawnee warrior kneel down next to his dead wife and child. The Pawnee man looked up and their eyes met for an instant. Hatred twisted the Pawnee's face into a horrible mask. He knew he would see this man again and they would have to settle things once and for all.

Gil Tomjack was tired of working the stolen cattle. It was hard work gathering up all those steers and driving them into the stronghold. He needed a rest so he rolled a smoke and walked over to where Black Knife lay.

'Taking a little break, huh?' he asked.

Black Knife looked up and shaded his eyes from the late-afternoon sun.

'Yes. I've had enough for now, how about you?'

Tomjack nodded. 'So what are you thinking?'

'Just thinking about Roberts and how he must want to kill me real bad.'

'I'm sure he wants to catch up with you in the worst way.'

'I never figured he would end up a damn sheriff, especially up here. But that's all right with me. I look forward to when he and I settle this once and for all. I don't like knowing there is someone out skulking around who wants to kill me. I don't like it one bit.'

'You figure once he finds out you're here he'll come at you?'

'I'm sure of it. He got a good look at me

and he will want revenge for his wife and child.'

'How are you going to kill him?' Tomjack asked. 'Are you going to use the Spencer or the knife?'

'I mean to get real close and use the knife.'

Black Knife pulled a ten-inch Bowie knife from the scabbard hanging on his belt. He fingered the razor-sharp blade and ran it against his smooth face.

'That ought to do it if you get close enough,' Tomjack said. 'I figure you to be a good hand with that pig-sticker. Most Indians are, I guess.' He stubbed out his cigarette on the tree. 'I guess we better go back to work. Harvey doesn't like slackers and if we don't get this load of cattle ready there will be hell to play.'

Black Knife stood up and shoved the knife back into the scabbard. He pushed back his long black hair behind his head.

'Harvey doesn't scare me, but I would just as soon not have him breathing down my neck either. If he pushes me too far he will find out he bleeds just like anyone else.'

Tomjack shook his head. 'By God, you are a mean one.'

Jake Appleton rode down Main Street,

stopped in front of the sheriff's office and dismounted. He tied up the sorrel and walked through the front door. Roberts sat behind his desk drinking a cup of coffee and looking down at some papers. He looked up.

'Good morning, Jake,' he said. 'I see from the look on your face that you have something on your mind.'

The big rancher pulled up a chair and sat down.

'No sense beating around the bush, Roberts. I didn't come to jabber about the cattle-rustling, not this time.'

'I see,' Roberts replied. 'If it is not the cattle then what is it that brought you all the way into town?'

'Oh, I care about the cattle, don't get me wrong, and I care about how you beat my boy. But it is you and Amy that's on my mind.'

Roberts's body stiffened.

'What do you mean, me and Amy?'

'The way I see it is that you and Amy are getting a little too close. What I mean to say is that I don't want you seeing her any more. It's not right.'

Roberts's dark eyes bored into the rancher's face.

'What do you mean, it's not right?'

'What I mean to say is that you're an Indian and she's white. Don't make me say any more.'

'Yes, I expect you to have to say more,' Roberts said. 'There isn't any law that I know of that says I can't pay her attention.'

Appleton squirmed in his chair and his face grew red.

'Damn it, Roberts. You know you can't go courting a white woman. That's not done around here. What will the town say? What kind of future would you two have if you ended up together? You don't want a life like that for her, do you?'

Roberts cleared his throat.

'You listen to me and you listen well, Appleton. First of all, I am not all that sure she is interested in me the way you think. She's a fine woman and a man would be proud to have her at his side. I don't care what people say or would say. I am used to all that. Being an Indian sheriff has taught me a lot over the years about what people think. I am as good as any man and better than most.'

'You are not getting it, Roberts.'

'How do you mean?'

'I am not going to argue with you over

106

this. I'm just letting you know that I am not going to stand around and let her throw her life away.'

'Sounds like a threat to me,' Roberts growled.

Appleton stood up.

'I am done talking. You take it anyway you like but the long and short of it is that you stay away from her or else.'

'I don't like how you said that, Appleton. "Or else" what?'

'You don't want to know,' Appleton replied. 'Just don't say I never gave you fair warning.' The big rancher turned and walked out of the office, slamming the door behind him.

Roberts got up and poured another cup of coffee. He walked over and looked out the window. His thoughts turned to Amy. He was fond of her. She was smart, strong-willed and beautiful. It had been a long time since he had thought about being with another woman. His mind wandered to a time six years earlier – a time when he still lived at the Pawnee Agency in Genoa. He had traveled with his wife and son along with the whole band to hunt buffalo on the Republican River. Everything began fine. They found a small group of buffalo but needed a lot more if they were going to dry enough meat for the winter. Even when they ran into a group of white hunters who warned them they had seen Sioux sign near by they were not concerned. They were many and besides, the Sioux were supposed to be on their agency miles to the north.

It wasn't until they made a major kill and left the women to skin and butcher the great beasts while they rode away to look for more that things went bad. He would never forget the sight of his butchered wife and son lying on the blood-soaked ground. The Sioux had trapped the women and children in a steep-sided canyon. There was no place to run and they had killed and killed. He had arrived too late, like the other Pawnee men. He found his loved ones lying in a heap. He knelt down and gently picked up his son. His scalp had been ripped off and a Sioux arrow protruded from the little boy's back. He stared at his wife. Her scalp was gone as well and her buffalo-skin dress had been ripped off He raised his face to the heavens and screamed.

'Tirawahut! Why have you forsaken me! I have lost all who are dear to me. I am a broken man!'

Then he saw the Sioux warrior on top a

nearby bluff. The Sioux waved two bloody scalps over his head in triumph. He would never forget this enemy's face – never. The man's features burned into his memory. There would be a time for revenge when he would find this man and make him suffer. Not now, for he must mourn his loved ones. But he would never forget.

10

Deputy Leggot walked through the door and sat down across the desk from Roberts.

'We need to talk,' Roberts said.

'Fine,' Leggot replied. 'What's on your mind, Rush?'

'I've decided to ride out to the Pine Ridge reservation and have a little talk with Agent Thompson. White Elk told me the beef ration was short out there and I think something is wrong.'

'Do you think the Sioux are stealing all those cattle?'

'It's a possibility, I suppose. If they are starving then it's a damn good possibility. No Sioux brave is going to sit by and watch his family starve to death if he can help it. I know that much.'

'When will you be back?' Leggot asked.

'I expect by late afternoon if I get started right away. It's not too far out there and I'd just as soon get started now so I can be back before dark.'

Leggot nodded.

'I'll watch the office while you're gone and make sure everything runs smooth. I have some wanted posters I can check out.'

'That sounds fine. I will be back as soon as I can.'

Roberts opened the cylinder on his Colt .45 handgun and made sure it was loaded. He grabbed a Winchester rifle from a rack on the wall and walked out of the office.

The black stallion's gait ate up mile after mile. Roberts loved the Pine Ridge country from the cedar-filled ravines to the sagebrush that dotted the ground in all directions. Clear, fast-running creeks surged down the ravines and into the bottom ground. It was fall and the cool air made him feel good to be alive. It wasn't long before he knew he was on reservation land. He passed about a half a dozen abandoned Indian lodges. Soon a small group of wooden buildings came into sight.

He reined in the stallion and dismounted in front of the main building. He tied up the horse and walked up the steps. He went in the front door and noticed a slightly built man sitting behind a desk. The man wore a rumpled suit and he looked old and worn out. The man looked up, noticed the badge on Rush's coat and motioned him to sit down.

'Good afternoon. My name's Cyrus Thompson and I am the Indian agent for the Pine Ridge Agency.'

Roberts shook his hand and sat down.

'My name is Roberts – Sheriff Rush Roberts. Glad to meet you.'

Thompson studied the man sitting across from him.

'An Indian sheriff, how interesting,' he offered.

'Pawnee, does that bother you?'

'Of course not, I'm used to being around Indians although I must say I have never seen an Indian sheriff before today. I am a little curious as to why the local sheriff would make such a long ride out here to see me. It must be very important.'

'It is, Mr Thompson. You see there's been talk that the beef issue is coming up short. Given all the cattle-rustling going on around your reservation I felt we needed to have a little talk.'

Thompson leaned back in his chair.

'I don't think I like your tone, Sheriff Roberts. It almost sounds like you think I am doing something illegal. Surely you don't mean to accuse me of any wrong-doing, do you?'

'You take my question and my tone however you want, Mr Thompson, but I still need an answer. I need to know if you are cheating the Sioux out of their rightful beef issue. If the ration is short then I have to figure the Indians are stealing the cattle. No man in his right mind is going to let his family starve to death.'

'I can assure you that the beef ration is and has been just what it should be ever since I came here,' Thompson replied coldly. 'You can check the books if you wish.'

Roberts remained silent, then stood up and walked towards the door. He stopped and turned around.

'I appreciate your time and if you say the issue's right, then so be it. But just so we understand each other, Mr Thompson. I figure you're telling me the truth but you understand I have to look into all the possibilities. It's my job. On the other hand

I mean to find out what is going on and if I find you have anything to do with this problem ... well, let's just leave it at that.'

Roberts turned and walked out the front door. Through the front window Thompson watched the lanky sheriff walk down the steps and mount his horse. Damn it, he thought to himself. This nosy sheriff is going to be a problem. He needed time to think.

Thompson turned round and sat back down at his desk. He didn't like what had just happened. The last thing he needed was Roberts sticking his nose into his affairs. He was making a fortune and didn't want it to stop, at least not until he had enough money to set himself up for life. He had always wanted to be rich and live the life of a rich man. It wasn't going to happen on his regular salary as agent so he had to improvise. It was a good scheme and no one would be any the wiser about it if he was careful. The only one who knew what was really going on was the bookkeeper and he wasn't going to say anything if he knew what was good for him. Just the same, he needed to watch him closely. He couldn't afford any slip-ups now just when he was so close to having everything he ever wanted.

Something wasn't right. Even though Thompson had gone out of his way to assure him all was good at the agency, Roberts had a feeling that things didn't add up. It was just a gut feeling – nothing other than an uneasy niggle – but all the same it was there.

Roberts turned the stallion south and was only a mile from the building when a solitary rider appeared out of a clump of pine-trees near the road. He waved for Rush to stop. Rush reined in and waited until the man came closer.

'Are you the sheriff?' the man asked.

'Yes I am. Who might you be?' Roberts asked.

The man reached out his hand.

'Myron Doby,' he replied. 'I work for Mr Thompson doing the book work for the agency.'

Roberts shook his outstretched hand.

'I see. What can I do for you, Mr Doby?'

Doby looked back at the agency and then at Roberts.

'We need to get off the road. I don't want him to see us talking.'

'You mean Thompson?' Roberts asked.

'Yes. What I have to tell you puts me in a lot of danger.'

'Fair enough,' Roberts replied. 'Let's ride down in to that draw and you can tell me what's on your mind.'

They rode about a hundred yards and veered off into a small draw ravine protected by pine-trees and scrub-oaks.

'Let me make this plain and simple,' Doby began. 'Thompson is cheating the Indians on their beef ration.' He waited to see the sheriff's reaction.

Roberts rubbed his chin.

'Are you sure?' he said. 'I've heard stories that this might be going on but I don't have any proof. Tell me more.'

'It's been eating at me for sometime but I have to be careful. Like I said, I do the bookkeeping but Thompson pretty much tells me what to do. Here is how it works. He tells the government that he buys so many cattle at a certain price. He sends them a bill and they pay based on the bill, but he doesn't buy all the cattle he tells them he does. He buys fewer cattle than on the invoice and pockets the difference.'

'How long has this been going on?' Roberts asked.

'About seven months, I reckon.'

'Does he pay you to keep your mouth shut?'

'He doesn't pay me a dime because I don't want any money from that type of thing. He told me that he would make things rough for me if I ever told anyone what was going on. I was scared and until right now I haven't said anything.'

'So why tell me? If this is true your life could be in danger. Thompson won't want to be exposed and could do anything to prevent it.'

Doby thought for a moment.

'Sheriff, I am an honest man and I see the Indians are starving. The bigwigs in Washington took away their way of life and put them on this land. They don't know how to farm and besides the land around here on the reservation isn't any good for growing crops. On top of that Thompson is shorting the beef issue. It's not right and I don't want any part of it. Something needs to be done. That's why I flagged you down. I figured the only way to stop it was to talk to you.'

'Can you prove all of this, Mr Doby?'

'Yes, but it won't be easy. He has me run two separate sets of books. One set for the government that shows everything being done properly, but also a secret set of books that shows how he is stealing all this money at the Indians' expense. You have to believe me.'

'I appreciate your honesty and I believe you, Mr Doby. This is very serious and I can't let Thompson get away with this type of thing. He needs to be stopped. Here's what we'll do. You get that secret set of books. Bring them to my office in two days. Can you find an excuse to leave the agency?'

'Yes, I think I can, but it won't be easy. He watches me like a hawk but I will find a way.'

'Good. In the meantime be careful and don't give him any reason to be suspicious. I need those books to prove what he's doing.'

'I'll do the best I can. Two days it is,' Doby replied.

They shook hands. Roberts sat on his horse and watched Doby ride back to the agency.

Roberts reined in the stallion and rolled a smoke. He lit the cigarette and reflected on what had just taken place. So that's what it was – fraud and theft. Now he knew White Elk was telling the truth but one thing didn't make any sense. What about the cattle with the arrows in them? There was no reason for Thompson to kill them and let them lie like that. There was no doubt he was shorting the beef issue and pocketing thousands of dollars but why would he kill those cattle and try to frame the Indians? As far as Washington knew he was buying the correct number of cattle and giving them to the Indians for their beef issue. There had to be more to it, Rush thought to himself, but for now he needed to get back to Chadron.

Thompson stood on the porch and watched Doby ride back into the agency. The book-keeper dismounted and walked his horse into the stable on the far end of the ground. Thompson walked briskly over to the stable. Doby was removing the saddle when Thompson strode through the entrance and confronted the employee.

'Out for a ride, Myron?' Thompson asked.

'Yes I was. I find a ride quite invigorating. Don't you agree?' Doby replied.

'Yes, I'm quite partial to them myself, especially on a nice fall day like today. Say, you didn't happen to run into anyone on the road did you?'

'Run into someone?'

'Yes, another rider by chance?' Beads of sweat formed on Doby's forehead. He tried to avoid the agent's piercing stare.

'No, I didn't see anyone.'

'I see. Well, I was just wondering since I was expecting supplies in from Chadron. By the way, when you get a chance I need to visit with you regarding the accounts. Please come to my office later on this afternoon.'

Doby nodded his head.

Thompson turned and walked out.

Doby's body shook with fear and he felt sick to his stomach. He wondered if the agent had seen him with Roberts. He hoped to God that he hadn't.

11

Billy Appleton pushed in the batwing saloon-doors and entered the Olive saloon. His eyes slowly adjusted to the dim light in the smoke-filled room. He walked over to the bar and ordered a beer. He was still mad at Roberts for the beating he'd taken and wished he would run into the Pawnee again. Maybe he would see the sheriff tonight. The bartender set the beer on the counter in front of Billy.

'That will be two bits.'

Billy fished around in his pocket and tossed the money onto the counter. He turned and looked around the room. Then he turned to walk towards the faro table but he bumped a large man standing next to the bar. His beer sloshed onto the man's shirt.

'Watch where you're going,' Tomjack growled.

'It was an accident,' Billy retorted.

Tomjack's eyes narrowed. He didn't like beer being spilled on him.

'Why don't you shut your mouth,' Tomjack replied as he turned and faced Billy.

'You make me, big man,' Billy sneered.

Tomjack pulled his pistol and whacked Appleton over the head. Blood gushed from a jagged cut in his forehead as he fell to his knees. Tomjack hit him again across the back, knocking the man to the floor. He stood over him and waited for the man to stand up. Billy staggered to his feet, blood streaming down his face, soaking his shirt. Tomjack raised the pistol one more time but felt someone grab his wrist. A powerful arm spun him around and he was face to face with Rush Roberts. Roberts had entered the saloon just in time to see Tomjack clout Billy Appleton over the head with his pistol.

He had hurried over and just when Tomjack was going to hit the man another time Rush grabbed his wrist.

'Drop the gun,' Rush ordered. 'I don't know what the problem is between you two but that's the end of it.'

Tomjack stared at the lawman, his face red with anger.

'I'm just teaching him some manners, Sheriff. He spilled beer on me and we had words. It's none of your business.'

'I'm making it my business. You can't pistol-whip a man to death over some spilled beer. Drop the gun. I won't ask again.'

Tomjack reluctantly dropped the gun.

'I won't take this from a stinking Indian even if you are the sheriff,' he said. 'Leave me alone.' He took a step towards the sheriff, his fists clenched.

Roberts stood his ground. The man was drunk and things could get out of hand quickly.

'Easy, big man. No one wants trouble but you're under arrest until I sort all this out.'

'Like hell I am!' Tomjack growled. 'You aren't man enough to arrest me. I'm going to break your back with my bare hands.'

Tomjack suddenly turned toward Roberts with an uncommon ability for a big man, lifting his boot as he came. Tomjack's boot looked huge as it swung toward Roberts' ribs and Rush knew if it connected the fight was over. Roberts jumped away, scattering tables and people in every direction. The tactic worked, carrying him well past Tomjack's boot.

Tomjack advanced, snarling a murderous oath as he rushed forward. Balancing lightly on the balls of his feet Roberts waited, coldly inviting the big man to make his next move. Tomjack took the bait. Cocking his massive fist he ran forward and threw a haymaker that would have demolished a stone wall if it had landed, but it never did.

Roberts ducked under the blow and sank his fist clean up to his elbow into Tomjack's paunch. Tomjack's mouth popped open and a roaring whoosh of air burst forth. He doubled over and clutched his gut in agony while Roberts wound up and exploded two more punches on his chin. Dazed, Tomjack shook his head, sucking in great gulps of air.

But he didn't fall.

For a moment Rush couldn't believe it. Nobody had ever taken those punches and kept their feet. He was beginning to get worried.

Shifting his attack, Rush kicked Tomjack

square in the kneecap. There was a loud crack and Tomjack let out a whimpering cry of pain. When he fell to his knees, Rush clouted him dead-centre between the eyes. Tomjack fell back over backwards, his crippled leg collapsing under him.

But Tomjack had more left in him. He shook his head, trying to clear the pin-wheeling lights bursting in his eyes.

Roberts had seen men take punishment in his time but never this badly. There was something unnatural about it. Holding off now was out of the question. Tomjack was dangerous as long as he could move. More than one man had gotten his brain scrambled by backing away before a fight was finished.

Stepping close to the downed man Rush swung his leg and kicked Tomjack in the head. The blow nearly tore Tomjack's jaw off and his skull bounced off the floor. Then a shudder went through his massive frame and his eyes rolled back into his head. Seconds later his eyes closed and he settled on the sawdust-covered floor.

He was out cold.

Roberts steadied himself against the bar counter breathing hard but still full of fight. When he turned his eyes glowed and his glare raked the room.

'Anybody else want a taste of what he got?'

The fight was over.

Deputy Leggot had just poured himself a cup of hot coffee when Steve Harvey walked through the front door of the jail. Harvey nodded at the deputy.

'Roberts in this morning?' he asked.

'He's in the back checking on the prisoner.' Leggot replied. 'He should be back in a minute.'

'Good, I'll wait.' Harvey responded.

Moments later Roberts came into the room.

'I came to bail out my employee, Sheriff.'

'He works for you?' Roberts asked.

'His name's Gil Tomjack and yes he works for me. He takes care of several of my business interests.'

'Well, he's not doing too good this morning. I expect you might be able to roust him out this afternoon.'

'I see. I understand you beat him up pretty good last night over at the Olive.'

'I don't know if you know what happened but he had it coming,' Roberts acknowledged.

124

'No, I don't really know other than that you and him went at it pretty good. Why don't you fill me in as to what happened.'

'Not much to tell. I came into the saloon just in time to see your man pistol-whipping Billy Appleton. I told him that was enough and he took it personal. He came at me and we had a little dance. He's one strong man. It was all I could do to subdue him. Anyway, I don't see any problem with your bailing him out. Come back this afternoon and in the meantime I will get the paper work ready.'

'I appreciate it, Sheriff. He's a good employee but I know how he can get when he's been drinking,' Harvey admitted. 'Say, before I forget. Any luck on catching those rustlers yet? Talk is around town the Sioux are doing the stealing,' Harvey probed.

Roberts stared at Harvey for a moment before replying.

'I'm getting closer. I suspect it could be them but I don't have any proof yet.'

'Well, good luck. I'm sure you will find the thieves before too long.'

With that being said, Harvey turned and walked out the door. Roberts turned to Leggot.

'That was a little strange, Harvey asking

about the rustlers and all.'

Leggot looked up from the desk. 'It's big news around town,' he commented. 'He probably just wanted to follow up on the rumors. You know how people are.'

'Maybe,' Rush replied.

'Anyway, I'm sorry I wasn't there to help last night. I had my hands full down at the Silver Dollar. A couple of gents were causing a ruckus over one of Madam Bishop's girls so I had to escort them out of town. It must have been one heck of a fight.'

Roberts sighed. 'Yes, I guess it was. He's one tough *hombre*. Billy got it pretty good up side the head and I think Tomjack would have killed him if I hadn't arrived in time.'

Roberts looked up at the clock.

'I think I'll go down to the café and have some breakfast,' he said. 'I should be back in an hour or so.'

'Sounds fine to me. I'll see you a little later.'

Roberts was finishing his breakfast when Jake and Amy Appleton entered the café. Roberts couldn't help but notice how lovely Amy looked when they came through the door. They walked over to his table.

'Good morning, Sheriff. I hope you don't

mind us interrupting your breakfast,' Jake offered. Amy smiled warmly at Roberts.

Roberts pushed his plate away and took a sip of coffee.

'No, sit down. I was just finishing. What can I do for you this morning?'

'This is hard for me but I came to thank you for what you did last night. I hear if it hadn't been for you my son might have been hurt worse or even killed. I just want you to know that I appreciate it.'

Roberts's eyebrows lifted.

'Thanks, Mr Appleton. I don't know what happened before I came in but there was no call for Tomjack to beat your boy with a pistol. I won't stand for rude behaviour in my town. How's Billy doing?'

'He's got a pretty bad cut on his head and a heck of a headache but he'll be all right. I'm getting him from the doc's this morning.'

Amy offered her hand to Roberts.

'I want to thank you too, Sheriff Roberts. I know Billy can be a handful but from what I understand he didn't start what happened last night.'

She smiled again. Roberts shook her hand. It was soft and warm.

'Anyway,' Jake continued. 'I might have

127

figured you all wrong. Any luck on finding the rustlers?'

'No, but I'm getting closer,' Roberts replied. 'I can't say right now but I figure it won't be long before we know.'

Jake nodded. 'That's good. I'm glad to hear it. So far I've kept the other ranchers in check but time is running out. It has to stop before all hell breaks loose, but I think you know that.'

'Yeah, I know,' Roberts said quietly.

Jake and Amy stood up and turned to leave but not before Amy glanced back at Roberts. Her eyes caught his for a brief moment. A warm feeling came over him, something he hadn't felt for years. He wanted to see Amy again and hoped it would be soon.

Harvey was so mad he could spit nails. He glowered at the man sitting in front of him. Tomjack held his head with both hands and groaned. His head hurt. In fact his whole body hurt from the beating Roberts gave him.

'What the hell were you thinking, Gil? What do you do? You go out and get all liquored up and start a fight with some lunkhead and then on top of that you get into it with the sheriff. Serves you right to get a beating for being stupid. You won't be any good to me for a couple of days,' Harvey said angrily.

Tomjack looked up and replied through swollen lips.

'Leave me alone. Can't you see I'm all broke up. That sheriff's tougher than I thought. I'm going to kill him the next chance I get for what he done to me.'

'Shut up,' Harvey replied. 'You have a job to do and I don't want you going after that sheriff. Let me worry about him. He doesn't have a clue about our operation and I want it to stay that way. For all he knows it's the Sioux up on the reservation stealing the cattle and that's fine with me. Now, you better heal up quick because we have to move cattle. I just received a big order from Chicago and they pay top dollar. Get down to the stronghold and tell Black Knife that we need another three hundred head.'

Tomjack staggered to his feet.

'I'll do my job so don't go on about it but when I'm done nothing's going to stop me from settling up with Roberts ... nothing.'

12

A cool breeze swirled through the valley. The leaves on the hardwood trees burned with brilliant hues of gold and crimson. His stallion loped along the trail snorting periodically with each new smell. Rush decided that afternoon to ride out and check the surrounding ravines again for any signs that might point to the rustlers. He saw nothing but a small group of mule deer drinking at a creek that meandered through the valley.

Minutes later he was startled to hear a voice call out from a bunch of cedar-trees. He pulled up and waited for the rider to clear the cover. He grinned when Amy Appleton emerged riding a sorrel mare.

'Hi, Sheriff,' she called out, a huge smile covering her face.

'Didn't I tell you once to call me Rush. You don't have a very long memory,' Roberts retorted, trying to keep a straight face.

Amy tossed her head back and laughed.

'Oh, that's right. How silly of me to forget.'

Roberts rode up next to the young woman.

'So, what are you doing out here this fine afternoon, Miss Amy?'

'Oh, I just decided it was too nice a day to be inside so I decided to take a ride. How about you?'

'I figured to check and see if anything was going on with this rustling thing. Nothing so far but I sure have enjoyed the ride and it just got better.'

Amy blushed. 'Now, Rush if I didn't know better I would say you were flirting with me.'

Rush smiled. 'You take it however you want but I'm powerful glad to run into you. Why don't we get down and sit a spell. I'd like to get to know you better.'

Amy nodded her head in agreement.

'Let's do just that. I don't know you very well either and I would like that to change.'

They rode down the ravine and stopped next to the creek. He dismounted and helped her down from her horse.

'Here's a good spot,' Rush pointed out. They sat down on the grass.

'So, tell me Rush. Have you ever been married?'

Rush leaned back and stared up at the sky.

'I was married once. Her name was Lights the Sky and we were very happy. We had a son and life was good. We lived at the Pawnee Agency near Genoa. I worked at the saw-mill but when a white man named Luther North came to recruit warriors to fight the Sioux I joined. It was good pay and although I had some close calls it went well. We protected the railroad workers from Sioux and Cheyenne raids.'

'You said you had a wife and son. If you don't mind me asking, what happened to them?'

Roberts sighed. 'It was the summer of 1873 and we left with the tribe to hunt buffalo in the Republican River valley. It was important to kill enough so we would have a good supply of dried meat. We didn't know it but the Sioux heard about us going and they gathered their warriors and left their agency in hopes of finding us. Well, they did and we were surprised. They killed almost one hundred women and children. I lost my wife and son that day.'

Amy put her hand on his arm. 'That's so sad, Rush. I'm sorry. It must have been horrible for you.'

'It was. In the beginning I had nightmares. They lasted a long time. I never thought I

132

would get over it but as the years passed it got better. It's funny how time works in that way. I don't talk about it much. I keep busy being the sheriff and that helps, but sometimes I wonder how things might have been if they hadn't been killed. But that's enough of that. What about you?'

'Oh, there's nothing much to say other than that I came out here because I love this country. Uncle Jake's good to me and I'm sure he will let me stay as long as I want. I keep around the house and such.'

Suddenly clouds darkened the sky and the wind changed. It was like that on the Pine Ridge. The weather could change at a moment's notice. Rush looked up.

'It's going to rain and we better find shelter before it starts,' he said.

Minutes later the sky let loose and rain fell in torrents. He and Amy rode down the ravine until they came upon a deserted cabin. He tied their horses under a clump of trees and they ran into the shelter.

'This will do just fine until it lets up,' Rush said, looking around the inside of the cabin. 'I better build us a fire to dry off.'

He found some dry wood and soon had a big fire burning in the fireplace.

After a few minutes Rush looked at her

and asked:

'If you don't mind me asking, have there been any men in your life?'

Amy smiled.

'Just a few but no one I would like to spend the rest of my life with so far,' she replied. 'The men back East are different – not like out here. I like a man who stands up for himself and has the courage to follow through on his convictions, a man like you.'

Rush looked deeply into her pale-blue eyes and said nothing. He peeled off his shirt and hung it on some sticks he stuck next to the flames. Amy couldn't help but notice his broad chest, flat stomach and muscular arms. His long black hair lay plastered down his back. A longing to be with this man stirred deeply with inside her.

Rush turned towards her.

'I know this is forward of me but maybe you better take off some of those wet clothes so we can dry them out. I promise I will be a gentleman.'

Amy looked down. She hadn't noticed how her rain-soaked blouse clung to her chest, revealing the outline of her full firm breasts. Instead of turning away she slowly removed her blouse leaving only her petticoat to cover her slim body. She moved closer to him.

'Rush, I think I'm falling in love with you.'

Rush took her in his arms. He crushed her body to his and gently kissed her. She kissed him back. They held each other tightly neither wanting to let go. At last he leaned back and said:

'Amy, I'm not much of a one for words but I know I love you. I've loved you from the very first time I saw you.'

'You have, even after I gave you that lecture?'

'Especially after that lecture.' He laughed. They kissed again.

'But what about your uncle; he made it clear that I was supposed to stay away from you.'

'I don't care what he thinks,' Amy replied angrily. 'He can't tell me whom I see or can't see.'

'But Amy, I'm not white. I'm full-blood Pawnee. Doesn't that make a difference to you?'

'Rush, you're a man just like anyone else. I don't care and nobody else should either.' She hugged him again.

'We'll wait out the storm, then you better get back to the ranch. Your uncle will be worried.'

She nodded. 'I suppose we'd better, but

for now just hold me, Rush.'

She laid her head on his chest and he folded his arms around her trembling body.

'I can do that,' he said quietly.

13

Roberts was anxious to see Doby again. The bookkeeper had promised he would bring the ledger-books that showed how Thompson was defrauding the government and starving the Indians at the reservation. It made Roberts angry and he was determined to expose Thompson and make things right. He sat impatiently on his horse waiting for Doby to arrive.

Ten minutes later the bookkeeper rode up and reined in next to Roberts.

'Do you have them?' Roberts asked anxiously. Doby shook his head.

'No, he made me put them back in the safe while he stood there and watched.'

'Damn it!' Roberts exclaimed. 'We need those ledgers. You have to go back and get them. I don't care how you do it, but get them. Without proof we've got nothing. Do you understand?'

'Yes, I understand, but I'm worried.' Doby said nervously.

'What do you mean?'

'I think he suspects something. When you left the other day he asked me if I had seen anyone on the road. I told him no but I don't think he believed me.'

Roberts thought for a moment.

'I don't like it. The good thing is that he doesn't know for sure that you've talked to me, but if he's getting suspicious he'll be even more careful. I don't want you in any more danger than you already are but I need those ledgers. Can you do it?'

'This has been eating at me a long time. I've seen the Indians starving and I can't just stand by and do nothing. I have to do it. We can't let him get away with it,' Doby replied.

'Good. Be careful and we'll meet back here tomorrow at the same time. Good luck.'

Doby nodded and rode away.

It was dark by the time Doby got back to the agency. After packing his things he stole up the back stairs that led to the office where the books were kept. He went to the safe and twirled the knob until it opened. He reached in and took out the two ledger-books. He quietly shut the safe and put the ledgers in his saddlebag. He turned to leave but stopped dead in his tracks. Standing in the doorway was Cyrus Thompson pointing a pistol at his stomach. Thompson glanced at Doby's valise and saddlebag.

'Going somewhere, Myron?' he sneered.

Doby looked down at the gun and then at Thompson's face.

'Uh ... no. I mean, yes...' he stuttered.

'Make up your mind. I'd say you're all packed to take a trip.'

Thompson pointed his pistol at the saddlebag.

'What's in there?' he asked.

'Just some of my papers, nothing important,' Doby replied fearfully.

'Open the saddlebag, Myron,' Thompson growled.

Doby opened the bag with trembling hands and pulled out the ledger-books.

'Hmmm ... I knew you were up to something. Ever since that day the sheriff was here. You were going to take these to him, right?' Thompson questioned.

Myron replied in a shaky voice, 'Yes, yes I was. I want no part of what's going on. It's not right and I need to set things straight.'

'You're not going to do anything of the kind,' Thompson warned. He motioned towards the door with his pistol.

'Let's go.'

'Where are we going?' Doby asked.

'Shut up or I'll shoot you right here.'

Doby reluctantly walked to the door and they went out on the balcony. Thompson suddenly pushed the bookkeeper in the back. Doby tumbled down the steps and lay crumpled on the ground, his neck twisted in a grotesque position. Thompson stared at the dead man.

'I guess I won't have to waste a bullet on you after all.'

He went back into the office, opened the safe, took out a stack of money and stuffed the bills in the saddlebag. It was time to go.

Deputy Leggot burst into the sheriffs office. Out of breath, he could hardly get the words out.

'Rush, you better come quick. They just brought in a dead man to the funeral parlor.'

'A dead man?' Rush asked.

'Yeah, I was doing rounds when a buck-board pulled up in front of Clay's and they drug out a man's body. They took him inside. That's all I know. I figured I'd better let you know right away.'

Roberts threw on his gun belt.

'We better get over there and see what's going on,' he said.

The two men hurried down the street until they reached the funeral parlor. They entered the building just in time to see Mr Clay come out of the back room.

'I hear you got a dead man back there,' Roberts probed.

'Yes, a couple of men from the Pine Ridge agency brought him in. They said his name was Myron Doby.'

Roberts drew in a deep breath.

'Can I see him?' he asked.

'Yes, but we haven't had time to work on him yet,' Clay replied.

Roberts and Leggot walked through the door leading to the preparing-room and saw a man's body lying on a table. Roberts walked around to the front of the table and looked down at the dead man's face. It was Myron Doby.

'I don't see any bullet wounds. What killed him?' Roberts asked.

'From what I can tell it looks like he has a broken neck. No other sign of violence except as you can see from the bruises on his legs and back it appears he might have taken a fall. Must have been an accident. I will do a more thorough study but that's probably what happened,' Clay explained.

'Sounds good. If you find out anything different let me know,' Roberts ordered. He pulled his deputy over to the side. 'I know this man. Let's go back to the office and I'll fill you in.'

Minutes later they were back at the office. Leggot sat down across the desk from Roberts.

'I haven't had time to tell you before but here's what I know. Doby was the bookkeeper at the Pine Ridge agency. The day I went out there to see Thompson I ran into him on my way back. He told me Thompson was cheating the Indians out of their beef issue. He said he could prove it because they were keeping two sets of books and he wanted to expose Thompson. I told him I needed proof and that he had to give me the ledgers. We were supposed to meet this afternoon so he could give them to me.'

Leggot thought for a moment.

'So you think it wasn't an accident like Clay said?'

Roberts shook his head. 'Doby thought Thompson was on to him, so no, I don't think it was an accident. I think Thompson killed him.'

'What about the books?' Leggot asked.

'If I were to guess, Thompson and the books are gone. He won't stick around with me knowing he was stealing from the government. He's probably already left for parts unknown. But there's something else.'

'What?'

'According to Doby, Thompson was sending invoices to the government for cattle he never bought. So even though he was shorting the Indians on the beef he sure wasn't stealing any cattle.'

'So?' Leggot asked.

'What I mean is that someone else is rustling the cattle and we still don't know who it is.'

'So what do we do now?'

'Thompson comes first. I'm going after him. He's got a head start but I figure if I ride hard I can catch up to him. I'm going to the agency to pick up his trail. You stay here and watch over things. Make sure those ranchers don't do anything foolish.'

'You can count on me, Rush,' Leggot replied.

Roberts walked over to the gun-rack on the wall and grabbed his Winchester 73. He made sure it was loaded, picked up his saddlebags and hurried out of the office. There was no time to waste.

It didn't take Roberts long to pick up Thompson's trail. Thompson was heading west and Roberts figured he was a good three hours behind the thief and murderer. He kneed the stallion into a steady lope and headed west. The big stallion ate up the miles. He was strong and in good shape. Roberts was glad he had the horse under him. It was about noon when he entered a sagebrush-covered draw.

A shot rang out and Roberts heard a bullet whistle past his head. He ducked down and spurred the stallion forward. He jumped down and yanked the Winchester from its scabbard. The shot sounded as though if came from some trees next to a creek. He moved from tree to tree, careful not to give Thompson an easy target.

'Come out of there with your hands up,' Roberts ordered. 'I know all about Doby and his accident.'

'You know I can't do that, Sheriff,' Thompson yelled back. 'I'm in too deep.'

'You either come out or I'm coming in. Make it easy on yourself. No sense dying over this. Sure, you're going to do time but that's better than being dead.'

'No, Sheriff. I figure you're going to have to come and get me. I might get lucky and take you down. Either way I don't figure to have much of a chance.'

Roberts worked closer until he discovered Thompson standing behind a tree. He moved slowly, edging his way through the brush until he was behind the Indian Agent.

'Turn around nice and slow. I've got you covered and I won't miss from here,' Roberts ordered.

Thompson stood still, his hands holding a rifle. Suddenly he turned and snapped off a shot. The bullet thunked into the tree next to Roberts's head. Roberts stepped out from behind the tree and fired one shot. The bullet took Thompson full in the chest. He staggered a few feet, a red stain spreading over the front of his shirt. Then he fell to the ground. His body jerked twice and he lay still. Roberts shucked the empty shell from his rifle and walked over to Thompson. He looked down and stared at the dead man. He didn't like killing but Thompson hadn't left him any choice.

He walked over to where Thompson's horse was tied to a tree and undid the saddlebags. He looked inside and found the

144

ledger-books. Good. At least he could set things right at the agency. As soon as he returned to Chadron he would telegraph the Bureau of Indian Affairs and tell them what was going on. Then he would make sure the Indians got plenty of beef. He wondered what White Elk was doing and thought how happy he would be when he found out about Thompson and the beef. He mounted the stallion and rode back to town.

14

White Elk moved stealthily through the pine-trees intent on the mule deer lying on the side of the ravine not more than fifty yards away. He stopped short and slowly notched an arrow to the cherry-wood bow he held in his right hand. The wind was blowing across the ravine and into his face. If he was lucky he would get close enough to get a shot at the huge buck. The big Lakota Sioux man took a step and froze. The buck sensed that something wasn't right and stood up, his long ears flicking back and forth. White Elk knew he'd better take a shot before the deer had time to run off into the undergrowth. He drew back the bowstring and sighted behind the deer's shoulder, aiming for the heart or lungs. He let the arrow go at the exact moment the buck jumped to one side. The arrow struck the deer but further back in the body than White Elk hoped. It was a good shot but not one that would kill instantly. He would have to track the deer.

White Elk picked up the blood spoor and tracked the mule buck. He crossed over a narrow creek and worked his way up one side of a steep ravine and down the other. The buck was running but enough blood stained the ground for White Elk to follow his trail. He stepped into a clump of dense plum-thickets and bush undergrowth. He picked his way through the entanglement and stopped. He looked in all directions and was amazed to see a narrow opening between two rock walls. He cautiously worked his way through the opening until it opened up into a secluded canyon. White Elk gazed around him, amazed at what he saw. If he hadn't been following the deer he would have never seen the entrance to the canyon. He kept walking until he saw the mule deer lying dead in the grass. He knelt down and took out his skinning-knife. He would skin out the deer and then explore the land.

White Elk was so intent on skinning-out the deer he didn't hear the man sneak up behind him. Then he heard the sound of a rifle being cocked and a voice behind him commanded:

'Don't move.'

White Elk remained motionless. Someone had a rifle pointed at his back and he wasn't about to give them an excuse to shoot.

'Black Knife! Come up and bring the horses!' the voice shouted. 'We got ourselves a trespasser.'

'Can I turn round?' White Elk growled.

'Yeah, go ahead, but first put down the skinning-knife.'

White Elk dropped the bloody knife and slowly turned until he faced the man.

'I'd say you got yourself into a bad spot, Injun. How'd you find the way in, anyhow?'

White Elk's face turned red with anger. He hadn't done anything wrong and he didn't like someone sneaking up on him.

'I was following that mule deer. I didn't figure I was on anyone's land. Even if I am that's no reason to point a gun at a man.'

'Shut up,' Tomjack barked. 'You're in big trouble.'

147

Black Knife rode up with Tomjack's horse. He glanced down at the deer and then at White Elk.

'Bad luck for you,' he commented drily.

'What should we do with him?' Tomjack asked.

'We better take him to the stronghold. Harvey said he was coming today so I guess we better wait and ask him what to do. But until he shows up we're going to have us a little fun.'

White Elk edged away from the deer. He knew these two men meant him harm and he needed to make a break.

'Whoa, there,' Tomjack warned, levering a shell into the rifle. 'You're not going anywhere.'

Black Knife got down from his horse and tied White Elk's hands behind his back, then attached the rope to the cantle on his saddle. They left half-dragging the captive Indian behind them. White Elk stumbled along, falling down several times only to be dragged on his stomach before he was able to regain his feet. Fifteen minutes later they arrived at a clearing. White Elk caught his breath but was amazed to see almost 200 head of cattle milling around in cattle-pens made of cedar-logs. Over a dozen men were busy cutting out steers so that they could be branded. He realized that these were the men who were stealing the cattle from the ranchers. Black Knife got down and untied the rope from his saddle. He yanked the slack end and White Elk fell heavily to the ground.

White Elk looked up at the Indian and snarled.

'If I ever get out of this the first thing I'm going to do is break your back.'

Black Knife laughed.

'I don't think I have to worry about that because I have a feeling you're not ever going to have the chance.'

He pushed the captive over to the corral fence and tied him to one of the fence-posts.

'Now me and Gil over there are going to teach you some manners.' He leered.

Harvey didn't like what he saw when he rode into the stronghold. Tomjack and Black Knife were standing in front of a man tied up to one of the corral fence-posts. It was obvious they had beaten the man. His face was swollen and bloody. His body sagged against the post but a rope kept him from falling to the ground. Harvey dismounted and walked over to Tomjack and Black Knife.

'What the hell is going on?' he shouted. 'Where did he come from?'

Tomjack stubbed out a cigarette on the ground.

'We found him just inside the entrance,' he replied. 'He was following a deer and happened to get inside. We figured to wait until you showed up before we did anything much.'

'Anything much? Jesus Christ, you almost beat him to death.'

'Yeah, he got a little smart with us so we decided to teach him a lesson, right, Black Knife?'

Black Knife smiled.

'Throw some water on him,' Harvey ordered. 'I want to ask him some questions.'

Tomjack grabbed a bucket of water and threw it on White Elk.

White Elk woke up sputtering. He tried to focus his eyes on the men standing in front of him.

Harvey stared at the Indian.

'What's your name? Where are you from?'

White Elk spit blood.

'My name is White Elk and I live on the Pine Ridge agency. I know what you bastards are doing,' he replied nodded at the holding-pens and the cattle milling, waiting

150

to be branded. 'You're the rustlers. The ranchers are blaming my people for what you are doing. Sheriff Roberts would love to know all about your operation. You better kill me right now because if I get loose I'm going to kill every one of you sons of bitches.'

Tomjack walked up to the Indian and punched him in the face. White Elk's head snapped back and he lost consciousness.

Harvey had to think. His whole scheme was based on the fact that no one knew of this secret canyon. Not only that but White Elk could recognize him and tell the sheriff who was behind the stealing. Now that White Elk knew the entrance and saw what they were doing he only had one choice.

'Gil, you know what you have to do. We can't afford to have him tell Roberts what we're doing. But before you kill him finish with these cattle. Make sure you dispose of the body where no one will find it. You know how I hate loose ends.'

Tomjack nodded.

'We'll take care of everything. You don't have to worry.'

White Elk slowly regained consciousness. His head and body ached from the beating

151

he'd taken. He found himself in a sitting position, his hands tied behind his back to a pine tree. His eyes searched for signs of the two men who had beaten him but they were nowhere in sight. He had to get away before they came for him. He gave a tug but his hands were tied too tight. He tried to get up but the ropes held him and he could barely move.

'Won't do you any good,' a voice called out from behind the tree. 'I made sure I tied you nice and tight.' Tomjack rode up and dismounted.

White Elk stopped struggling.

'I suppose you're going to kill me now.'

Tomjack looked down at the helpless Indian.

'I'm afraid you have to go. The boss doesn't like loose ends and he made it clear you're not getting out of this canyon alive. The only question is how you'll die. I've been pondering that simple question for a spell. Thought I would use the rifle, but that would be too easy ... too quick. Then I thought about giving you a gun and having a last draw because I don't figure you know how to use one all that good. Then I thought of it.'

He slipped a nine-inch Bowie knife from a

scabbard on his belt and felt the razor sharp edge. 'Yeah, I figure to carve you up a little and then stick this in your gut. Open you up and pull your guts out and wind them around this here tree and let you just lie here swatting flies. But I'm going to give you a chance. I don't figure it's much of a chance because I'm pretty good with this knife and you don't look so good.'

Tomjack walked behind the captive and cut the ropes holding White Elk to the tree. He stepped in front of the Indian and crouched, swinging the knife back and forth. White Elk waited until Tomjack got a little closer, then swung his leg up and kicked the man in the stomach. Tomjack doubled over in pain. White Elk jumped up and grabbed Tomjack's gun hand. They struggled over the gun until White Elk somehow got one arm around Tomjack's neck. He squeezed until the man went limp and slid to the ground. Satisfied that the man was no longer a threat White Elk leaned over and picked up the Bowie knife. He made a slit around the man's head and grabbed a handful of hair. He yanked as hard as he could. The scalp came free accompanied by a loud sucking noise. He snapped the gory trophy to make sure it was free of any blood. He should have killed him, White Elk thought, but taking his scalp was better than killing him. He snatched Tomjack's pistol from his holster and jumped on his horse. Moments later he found the canyon's entrance and carefully manoeuvred the horse through the winding trail until they came out the other side. He knew he had to get back to Chadron right away and tell Roberts what he had found out.

Black Knife sat on his horse and wondered whether Tomjack had killed the intruder yet. He hadn't heard a shot but he figured he would have used the knife. Tomjack liked using the knife and it would have been nice and quiet. He thought he would just go and see. He cantered his hose towards the draw where they had tied up the big Indian. He pulled up short when he saw Tomjack lying on the ground, his head a bloody mess. He looked around and couldn't see any signs of the captive. 'Damn it,' he thought to himself. He dismounted and hurried over to Tomjack. He was still alive. Tomjack's eyes fluttered open as he came to.

'Jesus Christ, Gil. You done got yourself scalped and let him get away at the same time,' Black Knife exclaimed.

Tomjack groaned and felt his bloody head.
'He scalped me. The son of a bitch scalped me!'

'Yeah, and he done a right good job at it. Of course, he is an Indian. He ought to have known what he was doing.'

Black Knife got up and grabbed his canteen. He washed off the blood and gore as best he could and took out Tomjack's neckerchief. He tied it around the man's head. 'There, that's about all I can do for you. I figure you'll live but it's not going to feel good for a while.'

Tomjack staggered to his feet. Black Knife helped him mount his horse and they headed back to the corral.

15

Roberts was having a quick lunch at the café when Ben Kingsley, Tom Walker, and Jake Appleton stormed in and surrounded his table. Roberts could tell by the looks on their faces they were angry. The ranchers all started talking at once. He pushed away from the table.

'Whoa. Just a minute, one at a time,' he said.

Walker pounded his fist on the table.

'We just got hit again – every one of us. This time they got over four hundred head. This time we tracked them until we got into Cussler's Canyon, then they seemed to disappear. No tracks – nothing.'

'That true, Kingsley?' Roberts asked.

'Damn right it's true,' Kingsley sputtered. 'We aren't going to take it any more. It's those damn Indians from the reservation. We're fixing to go up there and find out for ourselves. If we find them on Indian land we're going to settle it once and for all.'

'Just wait a minute,' Roberts replied. 'You're not going to do no such thing. That's my job and if you try to take the law into your own hands I will arrest you just like I would anyone else.'

'As far as I see it, Roberts, if you had been doing your job in the first place we wouldn't have this trouble. You haven't done squat and I know these men think the same thing. We've had enough of your sitting around and not doing a damn thing. We know what to do and by God we're going to do it,' Walker warned.

'I won't say this again, men. I know you're

angry and frustrated and so am I, but that doesn't mean you can go off and do anything you please. Give me a little more time. I'll ride up to the reservation and check it myself.'

'As far as I see it, Roberts, you're out of time and we're done talking. Do as you please but don't get in our way,' Kingsley retorted.

The ranchers turned and stomped out of the café.

Roberts knew he'd better find the rustlers before the ranchers did something they would regret. He got up and hurried out of the café. Time was running short.

Appleton stood and watched the ranchers water their horses behind the stable. He was just as concerned about the rustling but didn't know whether what they were going to do was right.

'I've known you a long time, Jake and by the look on your face I can tell something's eating at you. What is it?' Kingsley asked.

'Yeah, I am worried. I just don't know if we should ride out to the reservation. Maybe we should give Roberts one more chance,' he replied. 'If we go up and find the cattle there could be a killing.'

'Jake, we can't just stand around and let someone steal everything we worked so hard to make. No, we can't let that happen. We took care of our own long before there was any law in these parts and we can do it again. We have to do it again.'

'I suppose you're right,' Appleton answered reluctantly. 'I know we have to do something. How many men do you suppose we need?'

'I figure you're good for eight and between Walker and me we can mount another twenty. That should be enough, the way I figure it.'

'OK. then we better do it. Let's meet at Table Rock in two hours. Make sure everyone has a rifle and their handguns. I got a feeling we're going to need them.'

The ranchers mounted and rode out of town.

Sheriff Roberts checked his rifle and Colt .45 revolver. He was about to leave when White Elk burst into the office. His face was bloody. His lip was split and a deep cut over his right eye seeped blood. White Elk stumbled into the room and fell to the floor. Roberts ran over and helped him into a chair.

'Good God, White Elk what happened to

you!' he exclaimed.

White Elk moaned.

'White men in a canyon ... stealing cattle ... tried to kill me ... but had to tell you.'

Roberts ladled out a cup of water.

'Here, take a little of this. Slow down and tell me what happened.'

The big Lakota Indian gulped down the water. Roberts handed him a cloth to hold against the cut on his forehead.

'I was hunting deer near the Pine Ridge Agency. Wounded one and tracked him into a canyon I've never seen before, couldn't see the entrance until I was right on it. I followed the buck in and when I was skinning it two men jumped me. One's named Gil Tomjack and the other one calls himself Black Knife. I heard them call each other by name. Anyway, they tied me up and took me back deep into the canyon. I saw the whole thing, Rush ... the whole thing.'

'What do you mean – the whole thing?'

White Elk caught his breath, then continued: 'They are the ones stealing the cattle. They keep them in this canyon until they can change the brands. Then, I heard them say, they drive them to a railway-head and ship them back East.'

Roberts drew in a sharp breath.

'So that's what's going on.'

It all made sense. It wasn't the Indians and it wasn't Thompson. It was Tomjack and Black Knife doing the rustling. He directed his attention back to the Indian.

'Do you think you can find this canyon again?'

White Elk nodded.

'Yeah, I can find it. It's just south of Cussler's Canyon, hidden near the far north end. A clump of pine-thickets hides the entrance. We better get there quick. They were going to kill me. When Tomjack came to do me in somehow I got the drop on him. We fought until I got him down on the ground. Took his own knife and scalped him.'

He pulled a bloody scalp from his belt and threw it on the desk.

'Jesus, White Elk!' Roberts exclaimed,

'When Black Knife finds the bastard I'm thinking they'll pull out. He has to know I'd come straight to you.'

'How many men did you see?'

'I figure about a dozen or so,' White Elk replied. 'But I almost forgot. There was one other man with Tomjack and Black Knife and he asked all the questions.'

'Did you know him? Did you hear his name?' Roberts asked.

'Never saw him before. They never called him by name so I can't help you there, but he seemed to be the one in charge.'

Roberts thought for a moment.

'We've got to go back there right away but before we leave you need that cut sewed up. Go over to Doc Claiborne's office and get fixed up and then come straight back here.'

Roberts threw a couple of cartridge boxes into his saddlebags. He was just walking out the door when Deputy Leggot came in.

'Good, I'm glad you're here,' Roberts said.

'What's going on? I just saw White Elk walking over to Doc Claiborne's. He didn't look too good.'

Roberts filled him in on what was happening.

'White Elk and I are going back to the canyon but I want you to find Appleton and the rest of the ranchers. Tell them what happened. You have to stop them before they get to the reservation. I figure there's a dozen or so in that canyon and I'm going to need help. See if you can talk them into going there right away. Just ride to Cussler's Canyon and then follow the creek north until you get to a big clump of plum-thicket. That's where White Elk said the entrance was. I'm counting on you.'

161

Leggot nodded. 'I'll leave right now. I think I know where they might meet before going up there.'

Amy Appleton was standing in front of the café when she saw Sheriff Roberts emerge from his office and walk to his horse. She watched while he slipped the rifle he was holding into the scabbard on the horse. His face was grim and he looked as though he had a lot on his mind. She hurried across the street.

'Rush, what's going on? I just saw Uncle Jake and the other ranchers leave town in a hurry.'

Rush stopped and turned to face her.

'I don't have much time to talk, but I just found out the rustlers are holed up near Cussler's Canyon. They've been stealing the ranchers blind and taking the cattle into a secret canyon. White Elk and I are headed out there to arrest them. He was there and knows the way.'

'Just the two of you?' she asked anxiously.

'Yeah, but I sent Leggot to find your uncle and the rest of them. I want them to get out there just as soon as possible. We're going to need some help.'

'I'm going with you,' Amy said firmly. 'I

162

can shoot a rifle.'

Rush grabbed her shoulders and looked into her eyes.

'I appreciate it, Amy. But you stay here. I mean it. It's too dangerous and if anything ever happened to you I wouldn't be able to forgive myself for letting you go along.'

Tears filled Amy's eyes. She hugged Rush and held him tightly. Moments later she let go and stepped back.

'OK, I'll stay, but be careful. I know you can take care of yourself but all the same I won't stop worrying until you come back safe.'

Rush leaned forward and kissed her hard on the lips.

'I will, Amy. I promise. I don't want to lose you either. You know I love you. I'll be back.'

He mounted the stallion and rode down the street until he came to Doc Claiborne's. White Elk saw him coming and stepped outside.

'I see you got sewed up,' Rush observed. 'You have a gun?'

'Yeah, I'll use Tomjack's rifle.'

'Good. Let's go,' Roberts replied. White Elk mounted his horse and together they galloped out of town.

Amy watched anxiously as Rush and

163

White Elk rode away. She brushed the tears from her eyes and thought for a moment before a determined look came over her face. There was no way she was going to stay behind and let the man she loved face the rustlers with just White Elk. She hurried down the street to the livery stable and found her horse. She yanked the Winchester carbine from its scabbard and worked the lever action twice to make sure it was fully loaded. She was as good a shot as any man and she wasn't afraid to use it. Satisfied, she shoved the rifle back in its scabbard and jumped on her horse. She would follow her man and be there with him regardless of the danger.

Clint Harvey felt uneasy. He paced up and down with a worried look on his face. Even though they had eliminated the man who blundered into the stronghold he was still concerned. He couldn't put his finger on why, but the uneasy feeling was there all the same. His thoughts turned to the sheriff. Roberts was no fool. He was smart and not a man to be underestimated. Killing the Indian at the stronghold didn't concern him but if he had found the entrance to the canyon then it was only a matter of time before someone else did as well. He walked over to the wall safe and twirled the knob until it opened. He reached in and removed four stacks of currency. Rustling cattle was quite profitable, he thought to himself as he counted over $50,000 in cash. With that kind of money he would be able to buy all the political clout he needed to be the next territorial governor. Hmm ... Clint Harvey, Territorial Governor. Yeah, he liked the sound of it. Maybe it was time to stop rustling cattle before he was found out. He had all the money he needed so why take any more chances. He took another sip of whiskey and gazed out the window. He needed just a little more time for Tomjack and Black Knife to ship the last load of cattle, then he would call off the rustling. But one thing he did know. If Roberts got in his way he would kill him, then hire his own sheriff.

16

Deputy Leggot was sure the ranchers would meet at a hill called Table Rock about ten miles north-west of Chadron. He kept the bay at a fast, steady pace and the big horse felt strong underneath him. He was happy that at least they knew who was doing the rustling but, at the same time, he was concerned for Roberts and White Elk. He hoped they would wait long enough for him to bring the ranchers and their men to the canyon before doing anything themselves. But he also knew Roberts wasn't the kind of man who waited much when it was time for action. If they went in and found the rustlers there would be a fight and Roberts would be in the middle of it. As he neared Table Rock he hoped he wasn't too late. He blew out a sigh of relief when he arrived at the bottom of Table Rock and saw a group of men on horses milling around. Other riders were joining the group as he rode up.

He reined in, in front of Jake Appleton.

'Thank God I got here in time,' he said,

breathlessly. 'We need your help. Rush needs your help.' Appleton's two sons and the other ranchers clustered around the excited deputy.

Appleton glanced at the sweat-covered horse and handed the deputy a canteen.

'Here, take a drink and calm down. You ran that bay awful hard. What's going on?' Leggot swished the water around his mouth then spit it on the ground.

'Sheriff Roberts sent me to find you and the others. He knows who the rustlers are and needs your help.'

Jake slapped his thigh.

'By God that's good news. Who are they?'

'Gil Tomjack and an Indian called Black Knife. There was another man but we don't know his name yet.'

Leggot went on to explain how White Elk had stumbled on to the secret canyon and what happened after that.

'So it wasn't the Indians on the reservation after all,' Walker commented. 'I'm sure glad you found us in time. We were set to ride up there and take care of business.'

'Yeah,' Leggot replied. 'That's why Roberts sent me to find you. He said you better come quick to the canyon, Tomjack and Black Knife aren't the only ones there. They got about a dozen men with them and he's going to need your help.'

'Well then, we don't have much time to waste,' Appleton replied. 'You know how to get to this canyon?'

Leggot nodded. 'Roberts told me the way. Let's go. If I know Roberts he's not going to wait around when he sees those two *hombres*. He wants to finish this rustling and he's not a patient man.'

Jake Appleton looked over at Charlie and Billy.

'You two go back and stay with the herd. They need looking after and we have enough men.'

Reluctantly they nodded their heads. They watched Leggot and the ranchers whip their horses into a gallop and disappear in a cloud of dust.

Amy Appleton followed Roberts and White Elk carefully so they wouldn't see her, but close enough to keep them in sight. She was worried about the man she loved with all her heart. She had fallen head over heels for Rush and now he was going to enter the rustler stronghold and try to arrest them. She knew it would be dangerous, especially since there were only two of them. She also knew Rush would be angry that she had followed them but she didn't care. She could shoot a rifle and she would be there for him no matter what. Amy kept on their trail, determined to help when the time came.

Black Knife knew there was a fight coming. He sat on a rock sharpening his knife. Ever since Tomjack had let White Elk escape he knew Roberts would be coming and that was fine with him. It was time to settle things. He glanced over at Tomjack. The scalped rustler sat next to him, his back leaning against a tree.

'How's the head? First time I've ever seen a man live through a scalping,' he commented.

Tomjack groaned and gingerly reached up to touch what was left of his scalp.

'What do you think. It hurts like the devil.'

'Well, I reckon that big Indian could have sliced your throat just as easy, then you wouldn't be hurting at all.'

Tomjack pulled out his pistol. He opened the cylinder and checked the loads.

'I know one thing, when I see that Indian again he's a dead man. No one's going to take my scalp and get away with it,' Tomjack snarled.

'You'll get your chance. The way I see it, he'll be back with Roberts. Don't know if they'll bring anyone with them but it doesn't matter. I'm going to kill Roberts. You can worry about White Elk. In the meantime, you better post a guard at the entrance to the canyon. I don't want any surprises.'

Roberts and White Elk entered Cussler's Canyon just as the sun began to set in the west. Roberts looked at the sky.

'It will be dark soon. We better make a cold camp once we get in and do a little scouting. I'd just as soon make our move in the morning when we can see.'

White Elk grunted his approval.

Both men slowed their horses to a walk as they neared the entrance. Moments later White Elk held up his hand and motioned Roberts to stop. He turned and whispered: 'The entrance is just past those plum-thickets. Let me go ahead and see if they have a guard posted. They have to know we're coming and if it was me I would have someone guarding the entrance.'

Roberts nodded his head in agreement.

'Go ahead, but be careful. No sounds.'

White Elk handed his reins over to Roberts and disappeared into the thick underbrush.

He worked his way through the tangled thicket, careful not to make any sound. Minutes later he reached the concealed entrance in time to hear a man cough. He quickly crouched down and strained to make out where the man was hiding but the deepening dusk made it impossible to see. Damn it, he thought to himself. He knew he was close to the guard but was unable to see the man's exact position. He waited impatiently hoping the man would move and reveal himself. Suddenly he saw a solitary figure stand up and turn around with his back to him. The man was no more than ten feet away from where White Elk crouched and had no idea he was there. White Elk slowly and carefully stepped towards the man, his hand moving to the knife on his belt. He took out the knife. When he was close enough he grabbed the guard with his left arm around the neck and slammed the butt end of the knife as hard as he could down on his head. The man never knew what hit him and fell limply to the ground. White Elk took his pistol, dragged him over to the side of the entrance and covered him with a tumbleweed. Satisfied, he returned to Roberts.

'Just one guard.'

'Well?' Roberts anxiously asked.

'He's taking a little nap.'

'Good job.' Roberts grinned. 'Let's go in and find a place to spend the night. It'll have to be a cold camp – no fire. We can't let them know we're here.'

They rode through the entrance and made their way down a ravine and up the other side until they found a small bluff covered with pine-trees.

'This is a good spot. The trees will hide us but we're up high enough to get a good look at the corral,' Roberts observed.

They tied the horses to a tree but made sure to leave the saddles on just in case they had to move fast. Roberts yanked his rifle from its scabbard and stood still when a stick snapped somewhere in the darkness. He levered a shell into the Winchester's chamber and strained to see out in the inky blackness.

There was only silence.

'You better come out. I know someone's there,' he warned.

Moments later Amy Appleton emerged from the shadows.

Rush lowered the rifle and took her into his arms. He hugged her tightly and then drew back so he could see her face.

'Good Lord, woman! You want to get your-

172

self killed? I told you to stay back in town.'

She hugged him.

'I know you did, Rush, but I couldn't stay there knowing the man I love was putting himself in danger. You might not have ever come back to me.'

'I know, but this is going to get plenty hot even though I'm hoping your uncle and the rest of the ranchers get here in time to help.'

'Do you have a plan?' she asked.

'White Elk and I were just about to talk about that so go ahead and sit down. I'll get you a blanket. It's going to be cold tonight without a fire.'

Roberts went to his saddlebags and pulled out a woollen blanket. He walked over and draped it around Amy's shoulders. White Elk looked over at Roberts.

'Well, you got any ideas on how we're going to do this?' he asked.

Roberts nodded. 'Yeah, I've been thinking about it. You say there's a corral down there, right?'

'That's right, a big one and when I was there it was full of cattle.'

'Good, because I figure we need a diversion ... something to keep them occupied once the shooting starts.'

'What do you mean?'

'Here's what I want you to do. Just before sun-up I want you to sneak down there, open the corral gate and then stampede the cattle through the camp. In the meantime I'll get in position to surprise them. Hopefully the ranchers will find the canyon and come running when they hear all the shooting.'

'Sounds pretty risky to me,' White Elk replied. 'What if they don't show up? They have more guns than we do.'

'I guess that's the chance we have to take. I'm sworn to uphold the law and I've had a bellyful of this rustling.' Roberts thought for a moment. 'You know, White Elk, you don't have to do this. I'm the sheriff and it's my job, but it's asking a lot for you to risk your life. I'll understand if you stay out of it.'

White Elk stared at the lawman.

'That's a fool thing to say. I've come to know you and the way I figure it we're friends now. I won't stand around and do nothing when you try to arrest the whole bunch by yourself. No, I'm with you.'

Roberts smiled. 'I feel the same way.' He turned to Amy. 'Now, what are we going to do with you? I don't want you anywhere near when the shooting commences.'

'You may not want it but you're going to need another gun and I didn't come here to

174

let yourself go off and get shot. I can shoot just as good as most men. Count me in,' she replied sternly.

Roberts shook his head.

'I don't suppose there's anything I can do to keep you out of this, short of tying you up, is there?'

Amy looked into his eyes. 'I don't suppose there is.'

'Well then, we'd better try to get a little rest. Come dawn we're going to have needed it.'

Deputy Leggot was confused. There being no moon didn't help matters any. He raised his hand for the men following him to stop. Appleton and Walker rode up next to the deputy.

'What's the matter?' Appleton asked.

Leggot peered into the darkness.

'I'm not rightly sure that we're headed in the right direction.'

'God damn it, man!' Appleton snorted. 'We have to find that canyon.'

'I know it and I'm trying but it's so dark I'm getting a little confused.'

'Well, get yourself unconfused because all hell's going to break loose there and we have to get there in time to help Roberts and

White Elk. Two men against a dozen aren't very good odds.'

Leggot stood up in his stirrups and studied the landscape as best he could.

'OK, we need to head more north-west. Let's ride.'

He slapped his horse's rump and they rode off into the night.

Tomjack and Black Knife sat around a fire cleaning their guns. The other men congregated off to one side, keeping to themselves.

'You figure they'll come in the night? I'm not sure Roberts will even show. He's only one man and even if he brings that Indian with him it's two of them against all of us. He'd have to be half-crazy to chance those odds,' Tomjack pointed out.

'Oh, they'll come all right, but I don't figure it will be in the dark, too risky. I figure they'll come at us at daybreak. If Roberts doesn't make a play he's finished as a sheriff and he knows it. They'll come and we'll be waiting.'

Tomjack nodded.

'You want me to check on Johnson? He's been guarding the entrance for quite a spell.'

'Go ahead. Make sure everything's all right and come back here right away.'

Tomjack mounted his horse and disappeared into the inky blackness. He rode across the clearing and eased into the draw leading to the entrance to the canyon. He stopped and whistled softly. No answer. He whistled again. Still no answer. God damn it, he thought to himself. Johnson better not be asleep. He pulled out his pistol and dismounted. Leading the horse by the reins he walked to where the man should have been standing guard. He stopped and looked but was unable to see anyone.

'Johnson, you there?' he asked quietly.

No answer.

He tied the horse to a small sapling and searched the ground until he found the guard lying face down. He turned him over and saw a huge lump on the man's head. A wave of fear came over him. He knew that the sheriff and White Elk were in the canyon now and could be watching at this very moment. He picked up the man and threw him over his horse. Better get back to camp right away and tell Black Knife.

Black Knife stood up when Tomjack came back leading his horse. He walked over and looked at Johnson's unconscious body draped over the saddle.

'I guess we're going to have us a little

party,' he remarked, looking at the unconscious man. 'They're here and they'll be coming.'

17

Dawn was in the sky when Roberts awakened, but the horizon was dark with thunderheads. A dampness in the air warned of a coming storm. He quietly woke Amy and White Elk. Amy watched Roberts and White Elk stuff their slicker-pockets with cartridges. Then Roberts risked a small fire. After they had had a quick cup of coffee they doused the fire and took up their rifles.

Together the trio worked their way across the ridge until they came to a break in the pine-trees and could see the corral in a clearing down in the valley. The valley was surrounded with steep rocky formations and it was clear that there was only one way to reach the valley below. They continued making their way closer until they came to a rocky outcrop overlooking the camp. Roberts studied the terrain and was not surprised that the rustlers were using this canyon to hide the cattle. Besides the concealed entrance, the abundant grass and the creek running through the valley made it a perfect place to hide the cattle while they were changing the brands and fattening them up for market.

While it was still dark they studied every detail of the camp. The corral was at the far end, which was good. If White Elk could stampede the cattle directly through the rustlers' camp they just might have a chance to take them by surprise during the confusion. From what he could tell the rustlers were fast asleep in their bedrolls clustered around the campfires.

'White Elk, work your way through those trees,' said Roberts, pointing to the ridge that ran around the clearing. 'I figure you should be able to come out behind the corral. Go slow and try not to make any noise. It looks like they're asleep, but don't take any chances. I'll give you enough time to get down there and open the corral. When you're ready get those steers moving.'

White Elk moved off with a slight nod of his head and minutes later disappeared from sight.

Amy and Rush stood alone on the rocks. She walked over and took his hand in hers.

'I'd feel a lot better if my uncle and the rest were here,' she said apprehensively.

'Yeah, me too,' Roberts agreed. 'But we don't know if they've even found this place and if we don't do something pretty quick those men down there could get away, discover we're in the canyon and come looking for us. I can't have that. Are you sure you want to be a part of this?'

Amy thought for a moment.

'I know this is dangerous but I won't let you face them with just White Elk to help. I need to be with you and help all I can.'

Roberts squeezed her hand.

'OK, but you have to promise to do everything I say. I mean that. You do what I say,' he said sternly.

'I promise,' she replied.

'Good. Now let's get a little closer so that when White Elk stampedes the cattle we have a better vantage point. But before we go there's something I want to ask you.'

'Go ahead,' Amy replied.

Rush cleared his throat. 'I know it's not the best time but I was wondering if you would marry me when this is all over. I love you so much and I want you in my life for ever.'

Amy looked into Rush's eyes.

'Of course I will marry you, Rush,' she answered warmly, 'and this is the best time to ask, when we don't know what will happen to either of us today. Yes, I will marry you.'

A relieved look came over his face.

'Good, I will take good care of you, Amy. You can count on that.'

'I know, Rush. I know.'

'Then let's go. It will be daylight in a little while and we have to be in position, ready when White Elk stampedes the cattle.'

They climbed down the rocky outcrop and walked, half-crouching, until they reached a small plateau closer to the camp. They found a large rock to hide behind which would give them good cover once the shooting started. All they needed now was to wait for White Elk.

White Elk moved carefully down the hill making sure he stayed behind as much cover as possible. He wasn't sure that Rush's plan would work, mainly because there were so many rustlers, but he would do his best all the same. Besides, he wanted to even things up with Tomjack and Black Knife. Ten minutes later he emerged from some trees and found himself behind the corral. He made it to the fence and moved to the gate. So far as he could tell the rustlers were still asleep. Reaching up he unlatched the gate, then he stood up and fired his rifle into the air. The loud crack broke the silence and startled the cattle. They milled around the corral. He fired the rifle again. The cattle panicked and surged out of the corral through the gate and stampeded towards the camp. White Elk hurried out of the corral and ran alongside the cattle, using them for cover until he dove behind a large rock. He raised his head and squinted through the dust, trying to see what the rustlers were doing. Shots rang out and he knew the fight had begun.

'They stampeded the cattle!' he yelled. 'Get the hell out of here!'

The rustlers scrambled out of their bed-rolls, grabbing their rifles as the cattle bore down on the camp. Mass confusion and panic overtook the rustlers as the cattle tore through the camp crushing everything in sight. One of the rustlers tripped and fell, his horrible screams cut short when the cattle crushed him into the ground. Led by Tomjack and Black Knife the remaining rustlers stumbled up the sides of the ravine and fell behind whatever cover they could find. Moments later they were firing at the two figures hidden behind the rock on the high ground.

Amy and Roberts were firing their rifles as fast as they could reload. The rustlers fired back, determined to kill their assailants on the hill. Bullets cut the air around both Amy and Roberts and several ricocheted off the rocks. Roberts aimed carefully and shot one of the rustlers in the chest. He fell to the ground and lay still. Amy fired twice at one man and hit him in the leg. He screamed with pain and hobbled out of sight. There was no time for talk as Roberts and Amy fired until both rifles were empty. They grabbed loose cartridges from their pockets and quickly reloaded.

Suddenly the firing stopped and all was silent.

'I know you're up there, Roberts,' Black Knife yelled out. 'You don't stand a chance. I got too many men down here.'

Roberts slipped three more cartridges into his Winchester and yelled back.

'Give it up. We've got more on the way. Appleton and all the ranchers are on the way. You might as well surrender.'

'Well, I don't see them yet and you'll be a dead man before they ever get here.'

'We'll see,' Roberts shouted back. He stood up and fired two quick shots at the rustler. 'Get to fighting or give it up.'

Both Black Knife and Tomjack fired back at the sheriff. All hell broke loose when the rest of the rustlers also fired at the pair on the hill. Bullet after bullet struck the round and the rock they were hiding behind. Roberts yanked Amy to his side. He wiped the sweat from his brow.

'They have too much fire power,' he said. 'If your uncle and Leggot don't show up soon I'm afraid we're in big trouble. How many cartridges do you have left?'

Amy reached in her pockets and pulled out about twenty brass cartridges.

'That's it. How about you?' she asked.

Roberts felt around in his slicker.

'I don't have many more than that myself.'

Amy grabbed his arm and stared into his eyes.

'Uncle Jake will come. I know it. We just have to hold off a little longer.'

Roberts nodded. 'OK but only shoot when you have a good target. Once our rifle shells are gone we only have my pistol and they're too far away for that to be any good.'

Amy stood up and prepared to squeeze off a shot. She took her time and waited until a rustler showed himself before she fired. She missed but the man ducked his head from the close shot.

Black Knife turned to Tomjack.

'They have to be almost out of ammunition by now,' he said. 'All we have to do is keep them pinned down until they run out and then it will be easy. We can send the men around the hill and they can come up on them from behind.'

Tomjack nodded and fired his rifle. He squatted down to reload when the sound of heavy firing rang out from the far end of the valley. He stood up and saw twenty mounted men galloping toward their position, firing rifles as they came. It was Appleton and the ranchers. Before he could utter a word two of the rustlers were hit. Tomjack yelled at Black Knife.

'Here they come, God damn it! I don't know about you but I'm getting out of here! I'm not going to let them string me up to a tree for what we done!'

Black Knife raised his head and saw Deputy Leggot and Appleton leading the way. He knew it was time to go.

'Let's get out of here,' he screamed.

Both he and Tomjack broke cover and ran down the side of the ravine. Then they split in two directions. The remaining rustlers threw down their rifles and raised their hands in surrender when the ranchers rode up. Appleton looked up the hill and waved his arm.

'Thank God we got here in time,' he yelled up at his niece.

Amy waved back.

Before Roberts could acknowledge Appleton he saw Tomjack and Black Knife running down the ravine. He stepped away from the rock and took off down the hill in pursuit.

'Rush, wait for Uncle Jack,' Amy called out. 'Don't go after them by yourself.'

'I don't have time,' Roberts yelled back. 'They're getting away. Besides, I've got a score to settle with Black Knife!'

Roberts ran as fast as he could down the ravine and cut across the open ground until he reached the other side. He came to an abrupt stop when White Elk emerged from the trees. Roberts caught his breath.

'Both those bastards are getting away,' he yelled out. 'You take Tomjack and I'll go after Black Knife.'

White Elk caught a glimpse of Tomjack running down the ravine. He nodded and took off after the rustler. Roberts ran in the direction he'd last seen Black Knife.

White Elk gained ground on the rustler. When he was close enough he stopped. He raised his rifle and fired a shot at the fleeing rustler but it flew high. The bullet snapped off a branch over Tomjack's head and showered him with splinters. The rustler turned around and grinned at his pursuer. Before White Elk could shoot again, Tomjack disappeared into the thick underbrush.

'Damn it,' White Elk swore under his breath as he slipped two more shells into his rifle. This isn't going to be easy, he thought to himself. He moved slowly towards the underbrush. Tomjack could be hiding anywhere in the tangled mass of plum-thickets. Sweat beaded up on his forehead and his mouth felt dry. He looked in every direction but Tomjack was nowhere in sight. Suddenly he saw movement out of the corner of his eye, but it was too late. Tomjack ran out of the thickets and slammed into him. He knocked the Indian to the ground and White Elk's rifle flew out of his hands. They rolled around on the ground, each man struggling with all his might to get the upper hand. White Elk desperately grabbed for the knife on his belt but the rustler was too strong. At last White Elk heaved with all his strength and was able to stagger to his feet. He had just enough time to yank out his knife when Tomjack leaped on him with a savage cry.

The thick-chested rustler stuffed a thumb into the side of White Elk's mouth and started to rip downward against the cheek and jaw. To the Indian's tongue that thumb tasted like dirt and smoke as White Elk bit down hard, grinding the back of his teeth against the sharp pain as Tomjack worked at ripping his jaw off.

Striking out with his clenched fist, Tomjack knocked the knife out of White Elk's hand, then seized the Indian's upper arm in his grip. White Elk flung both arms around Tomjack's powerful chest, locking his free hand around the other wrist, starting to squeeze as he bit down all the harder on the thumb.

With a shrill wail of agony Tomjack popped his head forward savagely, smacking his broad forehead against White Elk's brow. Bits of shattered glass and mirrored light seemed to spin outward from his eyes as he jabbed a knee into Tomjack, again, and then a third time. He heard the man grunt with each blow, felt each strike shudder through the chest of the man he gripped with his arms.

As Tomjack cocked his head back, White Elk released his grip, the fingers on his free hand shooting towards Tomjack's ear, immediately snatching hold in time to yank back the head as the outlaw tried again to smack White Elk's brow.

At the same instant, he felt Tomjack's fingers close around his ear, digging and tearing. White Elk took his knife and swept it in a huge arc towards Tomjack's back. He sensed the blade drag along a rib for a moment before it plunged on through the taut muscle there in the lower back

White Elk yanked it free then drove the knife downward again, this time fighting to drag it to the side as Tomjack stiffened. The rustler's body went rigid while White Elk struggled to turn the weapon this way, then that, twisting the blade through the soft tissue below the muscle.

Tomjack pitched to the side suddenly and fell to the ground. He stared up at the Indian with glazed eyes as he took three quick gasps of air, then breathed no more. White Elk stared down on the dead man, his body shaking from the life-and-death struggle. He wiped the bloody knife on his pants and put

189

it back in the scabbard, then turned and walked away.

Roberts stopped running and stood still, out of breath. He listened and looked in every direction but Black Knife was nowhere in sight. He checked the loads in his rifle and waited. Suddenly he heard a sound behind him. He whirled and caught sight of Black Knife running up the side of the ravine. The lawman ran as fast as he could across the open ground and up the ravine. He stopped again near a large boulder. Roberts sensed that Black Knife was near. He lifted his head and studied the terrain. He was shifting his head to peer at a different angle when a bullet struck the rock within inches of his face, then ricocheted into the air. He crouched, hesitating. Would Black Knife expect him to move to right or to left? One thing the rustler would not expect was a shot from the place where the bullet struck.

Risking a glance, Roberts decided the only place Black Knife could use for shelter was a clump of plum-thickets about sixty yards away. He lifted the rifle and fired three fast shots at the plum-thicket, then moved off twenty yards in a crouching run. He took another shot. His standing for that shot was perfectly timed with a movement by Black Knife, but Roberts fired too quickly and the bullet missed.

Just then the storm that had threatened to move in broke loose in all its fury. Momentarily blinded by a flash of lightning that struck somewhere nearby, Roberts lay still, awaiting the crash of thunder. It came and with it the rain. It came with a roar and a rush. Lightning flashed and thunder rolled and reverberated through the valley. The rain swept across the ridge in driving sheets. Then through the downpour, he saw Black Knife.

Dimly visible, the Indian was running down the ridge one hundred yards away. Snapping his Winchester to his shoulder, Roberts squeezed off two shots, saw Black Knife veer sharply to break his line of fire, then vanish into a clump of trees.

There was no shelter on the side of the hill but Roberts was determined to waste no time. He rose and moved as swiftly as possible over the open ground to get around the trees.

A shot came from nowhere and something struck his shin a wicked blow. His leg buckled and he went down. But when he pulled his pant-leg he saw only a great, rapidly growing swelling. He had been hit by a rock knocked loose by the bullet. He hunched behind a sagebrush plant until the numbness went out of his leg, but when he started to move, it was with a limp. He had a cut and badly bruised shinbone, painful but not bad enough to stop the lawman.

There would be no let-up now. He was in a fight to the death and with an opponent superior to him in bushwhacking skill, and he must never remain for long in one place. Whatever else he was, Black Knife was a master hand at this business.

Roberts moved now, half-running, half-crawling, utilizing every bit of cover. Once a shot clipped a bush near his head, another time a bullet burned the back of his calf as he jerked it from sight.

He saw nothing at which to shoot. Apparently Black Knife was working with some scheme in mind. Suddenly Roberts looked around, and his quick glance took the wind out of him. For an instant he felt as if he had been hit in the belly with a stiff punch. Behind him was a wall of rock thirty feet high. He had been cleverly manoeuvred like a sheep into a cul-de-sac from which there seemed no escape. To go back the way he had come he must first advance, going directly towards Black Knife's gun. And that was exactly what Black Knife would expect him to do.

He was under cover. For the moment he was invisible to the hunter, and he glanced quickly around. There was a dip in the rock, a gully worn by water pouring down over the wall toward the depression at the foot of the rocks. He ducked into it and ran, bent over, straight to the wall.

When he first saw the head he thought it was a rock. It was still for a long time but after some time, looking past it so as not to blur his vision, Roberts saw the object move and rise. And Black Knife was standing there, just behind the swell. Black Knife started forward, his rifle in one hand, going towards the rock cliff. Roberts lifted his rifle and Black Knife was dead in his sights but he did not fire.

Roberts stood still, his rifle in his right hand.

'Black Knife!' he yelled, and thunder rolled like far-off drums.

Black Knife turned and looked down at him. There was no more than forty yards between the two men, and Black Knife's tall figure stood stark against the gray sky.

'So this is the way it is going to be, is it?'

Black Knife asked. 'Well, you've given me a fair chase.'

He spoke casually, but his rifle moved fast. Roberts tipped up the muzzle of his own rifle, caught the barrel with his left hand, and shot from the hip. Black Knife's shot was a split second too late. The Indian staggered, dropped his rifle and fell to his knees.

Roberts held his fire, but stood with his legs spread, rifle ready for a shot.

'Well, you did me in,' Black Knife said, spitting blood. He grimaced from the pain and struggled to speak. 'I'd like a smoke ... is it all right?'

'I shouldn't let you, you son of a bitch ... but since you've got a big hole blown through your belly I guess it's all right. Have your smoke but before you die tell me who you work for. Who's behind this whole thing?'

Black Knife's face gleamed momentarily in the glare of the match, the light showing his hard face, then he bent his head, shielding the flare of the match with his body. When he turned the cigarette was between his lips. He blew out a stream of smoke then staggered to his feet.

'You finally caught up with me, Roberts. Well, it was a long time coming anyway. God, it's been a long time since I killed your wife and brat.'

Roberts stiffened. His eyes narrowed and he gripped his rifle so hard his knuckles turned white.

'Yeah, I'll tell you who's behind all this. Clint Harvey ... he's the one.'

Something in Black Knife's tone was wrong, some sound, some faint suggestion of... His hand reached behind his back for the gun he had hidden in the waistband of his pants.

Black Knife's hand swung around in an arc.

Roberts fired, working the action as fast as he could move his hands. He watched Black Knife jerk with the impact of each slug at close range. Then it was over. Roberts heard the footsteps coming before she reached him.

'Rush! Rush! Rush, is it you?'

'I'm all right, Amy,' he said. 'I'm all right.'

18

Deputy Leggot, Jake Appleton and the rest of the ranchers were waiting when Amy, Rush, and White Elk approached them. Appleton had brought down their horses and was holding the reins while he waited for them.

'Have any trouble, Sheriff?' He grinned.

'No, nothing we couldn't handle,' Roberts grinned back. 'But I'm sure glad you showed up when you did.'

Leggot got down from his horse.

'Good Lord, Rush,' he said, 'I almost couldn't find this place. We looked for most of the night until we came across the entrance this morning just after sunup. We heard the shooting and came a-running.'

Roberts gratefully shook his deputy's hand.

'I never had a doubt.'

'So now what?' Leggot asked.

Roberts put his rifle back in its scabbard and pulled out his Colt .45. He snapped open the cylinder and made sure it was fully loaded. Satisfied, he put it back in its holster. He looked at Leggot.

'Before Black Knife died he told me Clint Harvey was the one behind the rustling,' he said. 'I'm going back to town.'

'Not without me you're not,' Leggot replied.

'I appreciate it, Brad, but I need you to stay here and make sure the dead rustlers are buried and the live ones get back to town.' He turned to Appleton. 'I would appreciate you helping Deputy Leggot all you can. Your cattle are scattered all over the valley but you have enough men to get them rounded up and back to where they belong.'

Appleton replied. 'I know I speak for all the men when I say that I can't tell you how much we appreciate what you done for us. I know we've had our differences in the past but I consider you a friend now and if you need anything just let me know.' The other ranchers nodded their heads in agreement.

'That's good to know and I'm not one to carry a grudge. Besides it appears to me that I'm going to be your new son-in-law.'

Appleton grinned and looked over at Amy, who blushed.

'Well, by God, that is good news. We'd be proud to have you in the family.'

Amy took Roberts by the arm and together they walked away from the men.

197

'I know you have to go back to town and arrest Harvey but be careful,' said Amy.

Rush took her in his arms and kissed her hard on the lips.

'I will. You stay here and come back with your uncle. I'll be waiting for you.'

She kissed him and tears filled her eyes as she watched him mount the stallion. She stifled a sob and could barely watch as her man rode away.

Clint Harvey leaned against the bar having a whiskey when the batwing doors swung open and Roberts walked into the dimly lit saloon. Roberts stood silently inside the doors. He stared at Harvey, his hand resting on his Colt .45. The room grew silent as all eyes turned towards the lawman. Harvey straightened up and turned to face Roberts. His eyes went down to Robert's gun hand. At that moment he knew why the lawman had come into the saloon.

'So, I figure you came for me. Is that right?' Harvey asked.

'Yes, we just had it out with your men at the canyon. Tomjack's dead. Black Knife's dead. The rest are either dead or arrested.'

'And you figure I had something to do with it?'

'That's right. You see, before I killed Black Knife he told me you were behind the rustling operation.'

'I don't suppose you ever would think he was lying?'

'No, I don't think he was lying. I figure a man who's about to go under wouldn't make it up. Do you?'

Harvey sighed. 'No, I don't suppose he would.' He pointed to his waist and continued: 'As you can see, I'm not wearing a gun. Why don't you take off your gun and see if you're man enough to beat me in a fair fight? If you can do that ... well, I guess that will be the end of it.

'Noticed you favoring your leg. Something wrong?'

'There isn't much time, Harvey.'

Roberts untied his holster and let it drop to the floor. He moved across the bar-room floor, wary of the bigger man. He swung a right hand that slid between Harvey's half-lifted hands and hit him in the mouth.

Harvey lifted a hand to his smashed lips and looked at the blood on his fingers.

'I think I'll take off my coat,' he said, 'because to judge by that punch it will take me more than a minute.'

They removed their coats very calmly,

they faced each other and Harvey doubled his fists and took his stance.

'Now, Roberts, I am going to kill you with my bare hands.'

The two men circled warily. Roberts was under no false impression of what lay before him. His leg was stiff and sore and was not in the best of shape after the long struggle at the canyon.

Roberts circled briefly, then feinted a left to the body. When Harvey dropped a hand to block the punch Roberts hit him in the mouth. The feint and the punch made one smooth, continued action. The punch jolted against Harvey's teeth.

'I'm getting tired of that,' Harvey said, and when he came in fast Robert's stiff leg slowed him. He caught a wicked right to the side of the face that rocked him to his heels. He was driven back by the weight of Harvey's charging body, and the bigger man's hammering fists landed to his head and body. Ducking his head against Harvey's shoulder, Roberts caught the other man's right wrist under his arm and clasping Harvey's right elbow in his left hand, he spun the big man off balance and hit him in the belly.

Roberts released him suddenly, then followed up with two hard blows to the head before Harvey could get set. Then, toe to toe, they stood and slugged.

Harvey's wind was good and he knew what he was doing. He bullied Roberts back into a table which broke beneath him and they both fell to the ground. Harvey smashed a right at Roberts's head, but Roberts rolled out of the way and caught Harvey's sleeve at the shoulder and jerked. Coupled with the weight behind the punch, the jerk took Harvey off balance. Roberts bucked him off and scrambled to his feet.

They fought bitterly, brutally, driving, punching, butting without let-up. Roberts's breath was coming in ragged gasps. He had to slow Harvey down. Roberts feinted a left and smashed Harvey under the heart with a hard right hand. He took two stiff punches but belted Harvey in the stomach again.

Harvey backed away and ripped the last shreds of his shirt from his body. Shrewdly, he could see that Roberts favored one leg. Bobbing his head to duck Roberts's left he crowded close and knocked Roberts to the ground. Deliberately Harvey fell, dropping his knee to strike Roberts's injured leg. Roberts grunted, feeling pain knife through him, sure the leg was bleeding again, for it was cut and bruised. Harvey swung both fists to Roberts's head and then rested his left hand on Roberts's chest and drew back his right for a final blow.

Roberts struck swiftly at the left hand. Harvey lost balance as his hand was knocked away. Roberts rolled free and got up. He was bloody and battered, his breath coming in gasps, one eye swollen from a blow.

Harvey struck him with a left, then measured him with another. Roberts caught his sleeve, stepped in quickly and threw Harvey over his back. Harvey hit the ground hard and Roberts backed away.

His leg was stiffening and there was a searing pain in his side. But he had his second wind and suddenly he felt good.

Harvey got up.

'I think you're through,' he said, walking toward Roberts. Despite the feeling that came with his second wind there was the knowledge that there could not be much left within him in the way of strength. He must win now.

Harvey, too, had been hurt. But now he stepped in and swung. Roberts slipped the punch and smashed a right to the heart. It was a perfectly timed, perfectly executed punch and Harvey's mouth dropped open in time to catch a sweeping left hook.

Harvey's knees buckled and he fell face forward into the sawdust.

'That's it,' Roberts said.

He turned away, went to the bar and asked for some water.

A scream brought him sharply around. Harvey was coming at him with a two-foot-long length of the broken table leg. As Roberts turned Harvey swung viciously. Roberts dove under the swing and knocked Harvey backwards. Then Roberts balled his fist and hit Harvey. He hit him once, then again.

Picking Harvey up bodily, he threw him, like a sack of grain, against the bar. Harvey slumped unconscious to the ground. Roberts staggered over to a table and leaned over in an effort to clear his head. Drops of blood were welling from his nose and there was blood in his mouth. He spat on the floor. His head was buzzing from the punches he had taken. The doors to the saloon opened and Amy walked in. She leaned over and picked up his gun-belt.

'It's over,' she said. 'I'm here now.'

She put her arm under Rush's shoulder. He leaned against her body. 'I'm ready,' he said. 'Let's go.'

Together they walked out of the saloon and into the bright sunlight.

This Large Print Book, for people
who cannot read normal print,
is published under the auspices of

THE ULVERSCROFT FOUNDATION

... we hope you have enjoyed this book.
Please think for a moment about those
who have worse eyesight than you ...
and are unable to even read or enjoy
Large Print without great difficulty.

You can help them by sending a
donation, large or small, to:

**The Ulverscroft Foundation,
1, The Green, Bradgate Road,
Anstey, Leicestershire, LE7 7FU,
England.**
or request a copy of our brochure for
more details.

The Foundation will use all donations
to assist those people who are visually
impaired and need special attention
with medical research, diagnosis
and treatment.

Thank you very much for your help.